Praise for **So I'm A Double Threat**:

"As soon as I started it, I didn't want to put it down! The drama, the boys, the backstabbing. You really know your stuff about high school. It was awesome because I know that so many girls have been in Megan's shoes. I hope there is a sequel and Alex is in it. He's the typical heart throb hottie all the girls would die to have. When the book was over, I was sad I finished."—Katie

"My Tia Deets gave me your book two days ago and I absolutely loved it! Started it yesterday morning and finished it by afternoon. I couldn't put it down. :) It was very entertaining and a very good read." –Leia

"Congratulations on your book. A very good read. I loved it. But you just can't leave me hanging!!! I'm ready for #2. I now feel like I can get mine published. Thanks for the encouragement!!!"—Sherry

" So I get home today and my mom just gave me a bag of 'lunch'. LMAO! So funny!"—Mario

"I like the part at the end when she exchanges yearbooks with Alex. That part was romantic. I would give this book five stars***** :0;)."—Jose H.

"Best book I've read in the school so far. My sister even liked it(: She would hit me every time I'd stop reading the book. I can't wait to read your next book:D."—Maria

"OMG. I love your book so much. Especially when Meg and Amy went to get the lunch bag. Ha ha ha ha ha! I thought that was so funny!"—Gaby

"Loved it! "So I'm a Double Threat" accurately chronicles the angst, distraction and experiences of a typical high school Freshman, Meg. The plot wasn't overly heavy. I sat down and read it straight through. There were a couple of times when I laughed out loud (haven't done that with a YA book in a while), especially the "lunch sack" part. That really took me back. I am looking forward to a sequel."—Jeannette

"I love this book. It was so easy to read and exciting. It's like crack. Once you start, you are addicted and you don't want to stop. I can't wait for the second book to come out. I'm going through withdrawals. Great story. Keep up the good work."—Sonny

"I loved this book so much. It has experiences that some of us have been through in our freshman year and I loved it when they talked to each other about problems and boys. It's just a nice story. I hope to read the second part of the book."—Flor

"It was a really interesting book. I can't wait for part two to come out. You will like this book if you like action, funny, or emotional books."—Jose C.

"I couldn't put this book down once I started reading it! As a 30 year old, I was surprised how much I got into this book. Maybe it reminds of my high school years or how I envisioned my high school years would have been like! I can't wait to find out what happens to the characters...please make it a series! Would suggest this book to others to read in a heartbeat!"—Naomi

"Your book was fun and entertaining reading!"—Jerry

So I'm a
Double Threat

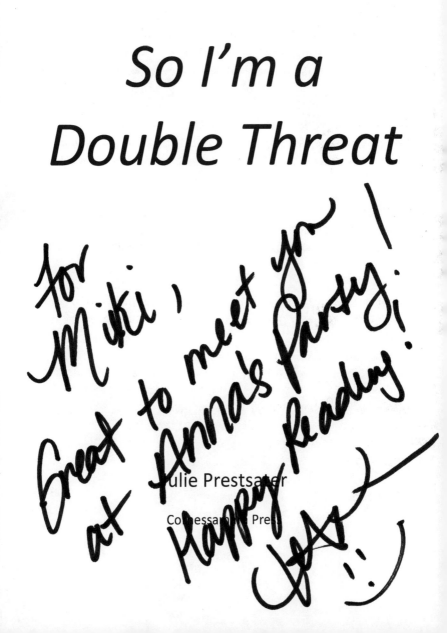

Julie Prestsater

Confessatary Press

Published by Cornessamara Press
California

ISBN: 1452863067
         978-1-452-86306-1

Cover by Daniel Van Beek of T-Graphics West
Concept for cover by Gerd Duerner

Photography by Adriana Pilonieta of Visual Imagery Photography
www.visualimageryphoto.com

Visit Julie on the Web at www.juliepbooks.com.

For my mom,
who read this book
more times than any one
person should ever
have to.

...
Thank you!

1

"A real...high school...party!" I squeal, in fear and excitement, while playfully shaking the arms of both Stephanie and Keesha. I throw my hands in the air. "Party over here...." I dance, as we stroll up the street. "Party over there!"

Maybe if I just joke around, I can calm my nerves long enough to be sane. Tonight is *the* night! We've talked about it every day since the first day of eighth grade. This is the night we've dreamed about. This is the night *I* have fantasized about. My heart is beating so fast, I feel like I can hear it.

"Heck yeah! No more junior high, seven minutes in heaven, crap. We're in high school now, baby!" Keesha exclaims, joining my dance.

I'm totally holding myself back from jumping up and down right now. I feel like I'm on a total sugar rush, even though I haven't eaten any candy since my mom rid our house of anything high in fat or calories. My mouth is actually watering like I'm going to hurl any minute. I need to calm down. But this is it. This is really it. This is so cool. And so freakin' scary!

"Okay Keesh. Meg. Try not to sound so lame. We don't have to act like freshmen just because we are," Amy snaps, as she clack clacks her way to the party...in heels. Yes, heels! People can hear her coming from a mile away. I think that's probably the point, knowing Amy.

"You guys better not get all stupid either. We've never done this before. Watch what you drink too! You never know...one of these horny boys might throw something in your cup," Steph cautions, always sounding motherly.

Keesh teasingly punches me in the arm. "Hey, Meggie! Maybe Alex will throw something in *your* drink." She chuckles, raising her eyebrows up and down.

My insides do a back flip every time I hear his name. "Yeah right! Besides I don't know if his sexiness will even be there," I say. I wish I could say I hadn't considered it, but I can't. Alex has been what I've really fantasized about, when contemplating tonight's party. It's been about Alex since the day I met him.

"He'll be there, alright. My sister is coming," Steph groans. Alex is Steph's sister's flavor of the month. I swear, Lydia changes guys like nail polish, so it's just a matter of time before Alex is chipped away, and I'm there to scoop him up.

"With the way Meg got all dressed up...she's probably gonna have to spike Alex's drink," Amy scoffs, looking me up and down like I'm a poster child for what not to wear.

"Forget you Amy. Sorry if I don't feel the need to show off all my Bs to get a guy!" I shoot back, defensively. "You've got enough boobs, butt, belly, and back showing to walk the streets," I continue, raising my voice to an almost full-blown yell. Does she always have to harass me like that?

"C'mon girls, calm down!" Steph says, loudly.

We continue our way up the driveway.

"Yeah, let's just chill okay," Amy says, pushing the door open to the party.

Keesh sticks out her tongue to Amy's back and turns to look at me. She places her hands on my shoulders and says in a determined tone, "Meggie, you look fine. Let's go in."

Yeah, whatever! I don't give a flying eff what Amy thinks anyway!

I can't believe the amount of people here at this party. As we make our way inside, kids are everywhere. Sitting, standing, and dancing to the music coming from outside. There are so many people that you just see bodies and can't even focus on any faces. It's all a blur. The dim lights don't help much either.

"This is crazy. Let's try to get outside...so we can at least breathe," Steph says, annoyed.

Amy leads us outside, weaving in and out of groups of people, paving our way till we hit the fresh air. It's instantly ten degrees cooler outside, even though it's still warm out. Inside, it was musty and gross, humid like a house with a swamp cooler in the middle of July.

"Hey chicas, it's about time you made it," Lydia shouts. She throws her arm over her sister's shoulder. "Oh, I forgot...you guys had to walk!" She slaps her thigh as she bursts into laughter.

Lydia gestures to some friends, then points to us. Within seconds, a few guys come over with red plastic cups full of beer. I think about what Steph said earlier, but take a swig anyway.

Ugh...why do people drink this stuff?

"Dang Lyd, how many have you had already?" Steph asks her sis.

She looks at her cup. "Who's counting? See ya guys later, I gotta go look for my man."

So Alex is here! My knees begin to go weak. I actually feel wobbly, like a baby taking her first steps. Maybe it's just the hot summer heat? It can't be the thought of Alex making me feel this way. Can it?

Meeting Alex at Steph's a few weeks ago is probably the worst thing that could happen to me just before school starts. I can't stop thinking about him. His deep voice and gorgeous eyes are enough to make any girl crazy. And to top it off, he's just so...nice. Every time I talk to him, he acts like he's known me forever. He doesn't talk down to me like I'm just some little kid, some little freshman, like some of Lydia's other friends do. It's different with Alex, once I start talking to him, I feel totally comfortable, like I don't have to try to be someone I'm not. I'm just me.

Ugh! School hasn't even started yet and I'm already googoo gaga over some guy. And not just any guy...a football player. A senior!

Suddenly, I awake from my daydream and realize I'm all alone in a crowded party and start to feel like an idiot. Amy tagged along with her sister, Jen, and her group of friends almost immediately after we arrived. Keesh went to dance with some cute guy, and Steph had to pee. I stayed behind to save our spot, a tall circular table full of purses and cups of booze.

I scan the doorway for Steph as I raise my cup to take a drink. Mid-sip I hear my name. I turn around to see Alex, strutting toward me.

"Hey Megan, wassup?" he says, with a grin.

Holy hotness! He's here. Right in front of me. Talking to me.

I set my cup down. "Hey, Alex!" I say, a little too excitedly.

I pick up my drink again, trying to gather some liquid courage to hold a conversation with this deliciously steamy guy.

"I heard you guys were going to be here. I was hoping I'd run in to you," he says.

This makes me even more nervous. My body starts to shiver while I struggle to hold my composure.

"Really...why?" I ask, trying not to breathe on him. I know this beer has to make my breath stink.

"I dunno...just to say hi, I guess."

I smile and I can feel my face turn red as it heats up.

"Oh. Well, hi!" I blurt out as I wave, like a dork.

"Hey." He smiles back and pauses, for several seconds. "So I hear you and your friends are gonna be in the ASB class this year." He looks directly at me when he speaks, something I'm not used to. Middle school boys do not look you in the eye.

"Yeah, we got lucky, I guess...Jen got us in."

"Are you gonna run for a student council position, or are you just a class member?"

I haven't thought about that. "I'm not sure, just happy we got in."

"It doesn't matter. Either way, you're a double threat." He grins. If only I could take a picture of that grin, I would have it tattooed on the inside of my eyelids.

Double threat? I'm confused. I turn my head sideways a bit, and crumple my brows.

"You know...you're in ASB *and* you're in Honors," he explains.

"What's that supposed to mean?"

"Hmm...let's see, ASB students can get away with practically anything and since you are in honors classes, no one would ever suspect that this sweet little girl with a 4.0 GPA would be at some party drinking...uhh, whatcha got in your cup?"

I smile. I can see what he's getting at. I put my cup down. I don't need it anymore. Like usual, once we start talking, I'm fine. It feels natural. The shivers are long gone.

"Uhh...just a little something." I smirk, looking down into my drink.

"Yeah...that's what I thought." He chuckles.

"So what are you then? You're not in ASB, are you?" I ask, trying to flirt but not so sure I'm pulling it off.

"I'm on the football team...so I'm even more of a threat than you are." He playfully nudges me in the arm. I feel like I'm in elementary school again and the boy I like is about to chase me around the playground. Alex is just so freakin' cute!

"So...dumb jock, huh?" I nudge him back. My elbow touches his arm and sends tingles throughout my body.

"I didn't say dumb, probably not as brainy as you, but..."

Out of nowhere, Lydia and Steph walk up.

"Hey babe, there you are," Lydia says, wrapping her arms around Alex's neck. My beer-filled stomach does a cartwheel. I think I'm going to puke. Nothing like a dose of reality to make me feel like I got punched in the gut.

"Hey Meg!" Steph yells. There is only one volume with her. "The girls are inside waiting for you...they're doing this beer bong thingy. They tried to get me to do it, but hell nah! The last girl that tried it had beer gushing outta her nose...Keesh wants you to try it."

"Oh...that sounds like fun, sign me up right now," I say, sarcastically.

Alex chuckles.

"Let's go for it Alex!" Lydia grabs his hand and drags him away, taking with them her foul scent of liquor. It's obvious Lydia is drinking a lot more than just beer.

Alex looks at me over his shoulder. "Later, Megan."

"See ya."

I continue to look at him as he walks away. He looks back again and raises one side of his mouth in a half smile. I quickly look away, trying to hide my giddiness.

"Oh my gosh, did you slip something into his drink Meg?" Steph says, jokingly.

"Shut up." I giggle. "He just came over here and started talking to me."

"That's cool Meg...but really, don't even think about it." She looks down at me like I'm a child who's going to get scolded. "He's a SENIOR!"

"He's a senior? Really?" I ask, kiddingly. "That's all you've got, huh. How about the fact that he's going out with your sister?"

"Yeah...I guess I should have something to say about that but I don't. Lydia is on her own when it comes to guys. Alex is way too good for her anyway," Steph responds. "But Meg, he's a senior. Let it go now, so you don't get hurt later."

"Don't even trip, Steph. Besides, who cares if he's a senior. Look at us...we're at one of their parties. We're in high school now. We're in ASB. We're in honors. We're DOUBLE THREATS!" I say, putting my hands on her shoulders and shaking her.

"What? Huh? Double threats?" Steph questions, obviously confused by my new high school terminology.

"Nevermind...let's hit that beer bong," I say, guiding her toward the house. "I bet I can win."

"The contest or Alex?" Steph asks, seriously.

I glare at her, and declare, "BOTH."

2

Can someone please tell me who in the heck gets to school early? Seriously, who does that? Apparently, me...I do. But not by choice. Since I'm going to be in ASB, I'm required to get to school early for Freshmen Orientation. Why? I mean...I *am* a freshman. What do I really know about the campus, classes, teachers, where the locker rooms are, whatever? How am I supposed to give other freshmen a tour or answer questions? I'm the one who's supposed to be a guest at this thing. All I know is that here I go, decked out in my new school clothes that are probably not good enough, about to walk to school in the hot August heat, hoping I will run into the football team since practices have already started.

Running into the football team would totally make my day. I haven't seen Alex since the big party a few weeks ago. It's not like I haven't thought about him though. I've seriously dreamed about him. I go to sleep picturing that grin he gave me at the party. That image is forever burned into my retina. He looked so hot, with an eyebrow hiked up and a half smile.

I just can't stop thinking about the party! Our conversation plays over and over again in my mind like the reels of a hot romantic movie of the summer. We play the Hollywood couple who can't be apart from one another. It's the perfect story.

I grab a granola bar (no more Pop Tarts in this house), a bottle of water, and I'm out my front door and on my way to Freshmen Orientation. Today is the day. Maybe, just maybe, I'll get to see him. Even though I had to wake up early, the idea of being at school today is not so bad after all with the possibility of seeing Alex.

I feel like such a loser hoofin' it in my beat up Converse, while carloads of students whizz passed me on my way to school. I recognize many of them, mostly upperclassmen, from that party. I wonder if they're in ASB too. They must be. Why else would they be going to school today, of all days, if they aren't freshmen?

This campus is huge. I feel like I'm being swallowed by its enormity. I slowly approach the student store, one meager step at a time, stalling, trying to shorten the length of time I wait by myself for my friends to show up. I look at my cell to check the time. It's eleven o'clock already and still, my girls are nowhere to be found. I knew I'd be the first one here, waiting like a dumb ass for everyone else to arrive.

I sit down on a concrete bench to wait, impatiently. My knee bounces up and down. I scan the quad. Still, there isn't anyone coming. I stand up. The blistering sun beating down on the benches made them scorching hot. The heat had pierced through my jeans and practically singed my skin. It's a good thing I didn't wear my jean shorts, or I might have gotten first degree burns on the backs of my thighs.

I flip open my cell, again. Only five minutes have passed and still no friends. I wait and wait, and just when I start to break a sweat, feeling moisture in the most undesirable places—my upper lip and straight down my butt crack—the football team decides to take a break and pass right by me. I happen to be standing next to the vending machines where they all stampede for a drink of water.

Oh crap!

Oh...my God!

There he is, full lips, big brown eyes, dimples, perfectly shaved head, and oh my! The sweat dripping from his bronze, tanned body makes his shirt cling to all the right spots. Damn! His chest is broad, muscular, and those abs—I can see that chiseled six pack right through his flimsy shirt. It's like my own private *Thunder From Down Under*.

If I had dollar bills, fives, even twenties, I would tuck them in, in all the desirable places to see more. I would lick the sweat from his body so clean he wouldn't need to shower for a week. Okay...so I wouldn't really lick his sweaty body...but I wouldn't mind touching it. Hmmm...hmm! Seriously...hold on...I know that is not the way an *honors* student is supposed to talk, or think, right? What would my mom think? I know, sometimes I get a little carried away.

Just a little...

As I try not to stare at Alex, I catch a glimpse of two long, tone, tanned legs making their way through the quad. I don't even need to look up to see who they belong to. It's Amy. She is the first of my friends to show. And boy did she show, or should I say show off! I swear, for as much money as her mother pays for her designer clothes, one would think there would be much more material involved. She catches a glimpse of me gazing at Alex, looking like drool is about to start dripping down my chin.

"Wipe your mouth, loser," Amy says, with a snicker, as she prances over to me. "It's only obvious you're staring at him." She rolls her eyes, while shaking her head.

Why does Amy have to get here right now, when all the guys are still around? Ugh!

The football players already started gawking as she sashayed up like she is on a freakin' runway. Of course, she gets the looks, the nods, the "hmm hmm, fresh meat" leers. Seriously...they sure as heck didn't look at *me* that way—I doubt they even looked at me at all. But then again, why wouldn't they stare at the tall blonde blue-eyed bombshell. Maybe if I plastered on as much make-up as Amy does, I would get those looks too.

I'm surprised Alex even notices me. He shoots a wave and a casual "what up" my way, after a lingering stare at Amy. Ugh! I wish he hadn't talked to me at that party. Now I'm obsessed. He invades my every thought, my dreams, and even my nightmares when I stop to consider that he is dating Steph's sister. Dang, this perfect guy is taken. Big deal, right! Like my size nine ass has a chance at him anyway.

But oh, can't a girl dream? Fantasize? Here comes that *Thunder* again!

"Heeeeyyy!" Stephanie shouts, ripping me from my dreams, letting *everyone* know she has arrived. She has to be a good twenty feet away but sounds like she is right in front of my face.

I begin to feel better now that Steph is here. I don't have to feel so...poofy standing next to Amy. Steph makes me look as thin as a supermodel. I feel bad for even thinking this about Steph but I can't help it.

We all give each other hugs, as if we haven't seen or talked to each other in years. In reality, we were at my house last night watching chick flicks, planning out our weddings to all the hot celebs.

It's not like we didn't spend the whole morning on the phone either, discussing what to wear. We didn't want to be too dressed up or too dressed down. We have a rep to protect. Not just anyone can get into ASB as a ninth grader. You have to be one of the "in" kids in junior high. You have to know people who can put your name on "the list". We were the *shit* in junior high. We know people. So, we have to get this right.

The guys are long gone by the time Keesha gets here.

"Dang Keesh..." I snap. This heat is getting to me.

"It's about time." Amy finishes my sentence.

"It's not easy to look this good," she slides her hands down the sides of her curvy body, "...*all* the time."

"Are you ever on time to anything?" I add. I swear it takes her like five hours just to pick out a pair of underwear. As if it matters which thong you wear when it's going to go straight up your ass. I don't get it! I spent my whole elementary and middle school years picking my wedgies. I can't understand why some of my friends act as if starting high school requires throwing away your hip-huggers or boy shorts in exchange for dental floss. I will definitely have to pass on the chafing feeling of thread between my cheeks.

"We've only been friends since kindergarten, have you ever known me to be on time?" she responds with a laugh.

"Alright, alright," I say. She has a point.

Amy and Steph have been watching us talk, turning their heads from Keesh to me, then back to Keesh like they're watching a tennis match.

Amy's the first to jump in. "Well, I guess it was worth the wait...you look good Keesh."

"Thanks Amy," Keesha says, with surprise.

That is a huge compliment, coming from Amy. She doesn't give them out often. Keesh does look good though. She has on tight jeans and a cute fitted top, a deep bright pink color that contrasts nicely with her dark skin. She has this classy way of looking cute without looking like a hoochie mama.

By the time we finish exchanging "hellos" and checking out what each other is wearing, we're no longer alone. Our new teacher, our ASB advisor, Mr. Mitchell, has arrived and corralled the class into the ASB room. The upperclassmen are all wearing school colors, orange and black, for the good ol' Carver Bengals.

I've been waiting to meet this teacher, the one everyone talks about. He's like a legend at this school. I hear he wears crazy outfits and dances around at rallies like a freak. The first chance I get, I take a good look at him. He is interesting alright, with bright orange pants and a cat tail coming out from his behind, and tiger ears peeking from the top of his head. Within seconds, he has the older students cheering, slapping hands, raising the roof, wooo wooo-ing.

"This is your year SENIORS! We're gonna make it happen! Rallies, dances, football games, track meets, whatever. This will be the most memorable year of your high school careers. Arrrrrrre youuuuuuuuuuuuu reeeeeeaaaaaaaddddddy?" he shouts.

"Yeah!" "Yes!" "Seniors, Seniors!" They all holler. The rest of us just clap in amazement.

"But first, we've gotta welcome the newbies! This year's freshmen class! Welcome freshmen!"

"Booo!" "Seniors, Seniors!" "Booo!" The upperclassmen yell, while some laugh at the same time.

"Okay...let's be nice to the kiddos! Let's not scare them away!" he yells, smiling and laughing like the others. It's all in good fun, but it's still a bit intimidating.

Mr. Mitchell continues with his speech. The energy is intense. Steph's parents, Carver alums, would be proud. The ninth graders, including me, have this kinda deer-in-the-headlights look on our faces, but we eventually catch on. We cheer. We yell. We clap. We yell some more. When we finally do start participating, Mr. Mitchell looks pleased. He quiets the class, starts giving out instructions, and delegating jobs.

The orientation itself is in the hot, stuffy auditorium—with no air conditioning. I go to a super old school. Don't get me wrong, the auditorium is gorgeous—I'd expect to see a Broadway show in a place like this. But today, students and parents shuffle in. Parents appear bright-eyed and nervous that their babies are really in high school. The freshmen hang their heads low, humiliated by the fact that they're walking on campus with their parents. Some freshmen are lucky enough to ditch the *parentals* and come alone, which is cool because they don't have go to all the lame presentations later on. They can take a quick tour of this *ginormous* campus, find their classes, and then just kick back and chill with friends. On the other hand, the suckers with parents are going to be stuck following the agenda minute by minute making sure not to miss a thing. Hallelujah, my parents had to work!

Being in ASB has perks! We don't have to listen to the principal drone on about rules and regulations. Instead, we sit in the back, making faces at each other, texting back and forth, and making each other laugh for no apparent reason. I can't believe people actually come to these things. I feel like I'm being tortured. The principal announces the counselors one by one. They walk on stage and just stand there, showing no emotion what-so-ever. One counselor actually waves, the others look at her like she's crazy. These are the people who are supposed to "counsel" us? I hope I get the one who waved, she's probably cool.

We all sit up straight and at attention when the cheerleaders are announced. They do a little spirit cheer, but the crowd is almost completely silent. The music starts to play and the rah-rahs begin to dance. They're pretty good, but a few are stiff and don't have any rhythm. It's almost painful to watch. But the others are so peppy they get most of the attention. Amy, of course, wants to join cheer. You can see the desire burning in her eyes. She is smiling from ear to ear and clapping every time they complete a stunt. Seriously, she would totally fit in. She has the attitude for it. All she needs is the tramp stamp and she'll be set—you know, the tattoo they all sport on their lower backs. She already has one picked out!

Keesha and I, on the other hand, get anxious as the dance team replaces the cheer squad on stage. We love to dance. We can sit in front of the tube all day watching music videos and practicing dance moves. The dance team is even better than I expected. They're all in sync with each other. They get into so many formations and never skip a beat. It's like watching a live concert.

I lean over to whisper in Keesh's ear, "We've gotta try out for dance. They're freaking awesome."

"I know, I wanna jump on stage right now...but they don't let freshmen on the team. We can't try out till the end of the year for next year's team."

"We'll be ready...I can't wait," I say, confidently. I swear, we're going to be up here dancing at next year's freshmen orientation.

Thank God! Orientation is over. I figured out where my classes are. Mr. Mitchell is pretty cool. My friends are still awesome. The upperclassmen are alright. The dance team was so freakin' cool. And Alex... his sweaty, sexy body, he's just...*Priceless*.

Carver High School...ready or not, here I come!

3

Holy shit! This crap only happens to me! I swear I set the alarm on my cell for 5:30 so I can take my time getting ready this morning. But, of course, my alarm never goes off and I wake up in a panic.

It's like I'm watching a scary movie and the bad guy jumps out to get me. I gasp, sit up, and my eyes pop open. My heart is beating so fast, I pick up my phone to see that it's almost seven. No way! School starts in forty minutes. Shit! Shit! Shit! I set my alarm for 5:30...P...M...—LOSER! Think fast, think fast!

So I jump in the shower, grab my loofah, squeeze some body wash on it and quickly swipe it all over my body. I throw conditioner in my hair—no time for shampoo—run my fingers through my locks, and rinse it all out in a matter of seconds. I dry off as I run to my room to get dressed. I squirt some mousse in my hair—it's going to have to be a curly, messy hair day. No time for the flat iron. A dab of mascara and lip gloss, grab the back pack, and I'm out. No one will notice I look like I just rolled out of bed, right?

Ugh! It sucks to get to school in a sweat. My legs hurt from walking so fast. I can feel the shin splints burning through my flesh. I get to the front of the bathroom, where they post the class lists, just as the first bell rings. Where the hell is my name? I pass up the A-F's. On to the G-J's. Okay, there's are the M's. Martinez. McMillan. Mester. Meza. And finally, there's Miller. With only a few Miller's, I find my name quickly, Miller, Megan.

That's me. Whew! My class didn't change. I'm in the clear. I already know where my first period is.

Crap! I forgot to turn off my cell phone. I can hear my ringtone, humming from somewhere in my backpack. I dig around for it, finding it just in time.

"Where in the hell are you?" Stephanie shouts into the phone. "I'm standing in front of our science class and I don't see your late butt anywhere!"

"Shit, Steph, I'm on my way…." A loud beeping sound erupts from the intercom. "Damn, is that the minute bell?"

"Yeah, I think so. You better hurry up! I'm gonna go in and save us some seats," Stephanie explains to me.

This sucks, I'm totally late on my first day of high school. I look like ass and I probably smell like it too after practically sprinting here. My legs are now throbbing. Seriously, why can't I go to a private school? This campus is sooo big, it's like walking across a college campus. It takes like fifteen minutes to get from one building to another, but you only get seven minutes in between classes. What the hell kind of crap is that?

Are you kidding me? Are you…kidding me? Seriously! I walk into class and the only seat left is in the front. Thanks, Steph! Oh frick, I'm gonna be stuck between Marvin Johnson and Lacey (originally Qian Na) Lam for the rest of the year. Kill me now!

By the way, why is it that Chinese people can change their name to anything they want? I can't just change my name to Sara or Samantha or anything else, for the heck of it. I'm stuck with Megan, or Meg, for the rest of my life.

Anyway, I kind of stare at the seat. I look at Steph in the back of the class. She scored an awesome seat next to some hot guy I have never seen before. Some chicks have all the luck. Apparently, I'm not one of them.

Mrs. Caldwell catches my gaze, and eyeballs the seat in front. I walk over to it quickly, as if I haven't already drawn enough attention to myself, with my fiery red cheeks, wet hair, and panting. I still haven't had the chance to fully catch my breath. Every time I inhale, I feel like my lungs are on fire. It can't get any worse than this!

"Good …morning… ladies …and gentlemen, …welcome …to …Earth …science," Mrs. Caldwell says in the most monotone, dreary voice I have ever heard. It reminds me of that retarded teacher in *Ferris Bueller's Day Off*, "Bueller…Bueller…Bueller". This is going to be a freakin' nightmare at seven forty in the morning *every day*. I doubt I'll even survive to make it to second period.

Well, it could've been worse. I could've gotten P.E. first period.

The rest of the day is the same old, same old. Introductions here, introductions there, passing out information sheets for parents to sign (first homework assignment, of course), and the inevitable icebreakers, as if breaking the ice is possible in a room full of teenagers.

How annoying is it that some teachers feel the need to be all touchy feely, "I care about you and your feelings", all "I really want to get to know all of you" crap, and the, of course, "if you need anything, you can come to me…I'm here for you"—what a load of bull! I swear if I have to play another game of "I'm going on a picnic and I'm going to bring…"—you know the one where you say your name and something you'll bring that starts with the first letter of your first name—I'm going to take all the picnic crap and shove it straight up these teachers…never mind, I'll *try* to be nice. Try.

I can't believe I even made it through the first half of the day: first period was "…Earth…Science…", second period was math (hallelujah)—Alegbra two 'cause I'm a genius—with Mr. Higgins, also known as the "Mad Hatter", Spanish was third period with Mrs. O'Brien—yeah, an O'Brien teaching me Spanish, I laughed at that one too! Next thing you know, Mrs. Apolinar Hererra-Reyes will be teaching German.

Fourth period finally arrives. This is supposed to be my kick back class—ASB! Mr. Mitchell is dramatic, just like orientation. I swear he projects his voice so loudly across the room, like he has a microphone. He is already in project mode, with the Welcome Back assembly coming up. Wow! Can you believe this craziness? We barely started school and we're already expected to plan a rally.

Mr. Mitchell should stop worrying and put Steph in charge. She will be good at this, she has the party planning gene in her family. I swear they always have the entire *familia* over for every occasion—seriously every "tia, tio, cousin, friend, nina, and nino" goes to her house for practically anything. Every day is a holiday at Casa Ayala.

Anyway, we're placed into committees, which totally sucks because the fab four get split up. Keesha and I get selected for the Activities, while Amy and Steph are slated for the Rally committee. All the upperclassmen say these are the best committees, and we should feel lucky. I guess I'm excited but I'd rather us all be together. I guess my mom is right, I still have some growing up to do.

Oh well, I'm over it. At least I still have Keesh with me.

Amy and Steph disappear with their group to plan the assembly. First, we reluctantly say goodbye to each other, severing the figurative umbilical cord that connected us. It's like someone cut off my hands, without them here.

Keesh and I follow the older kids into the cafeteria to hammer out details for the half-time activities for the first football game. Yes…did you hear that? Football! I get to plan something for the football game. I get to plan something for ALEX!

Oh my gosh! I can hardly contain myself. My knee is bouncing up and down at turbo speed. All these thoughts are going through my head. Will he see me? Of course, he will—he will run out of the locker room, onto the field, and stop in front of me for a good luck kiss before taking the field to run for the winning touchdown! Seriously, I know, I'm nuts! Sometimes my imagination runs wild. It's like a freakin' film strip running out of control. But really, wouldn't it be totally cool if that happened with Alex.

Like always, Keesh whips me back to reality.

"Ow…what's your problem?" I ask. She nudged me so hard in the arm I'm sure I'll have a bruise.

She shoots me an irritated look. "Pay attention, dumb ass. They were just asking you a question," she whispers.

I look around, but the conversation has moved on. I still don't know what's going on before the bell rings. That's okay though, I'll ask Keesha after class.

All that really matters is I'm one step closer to my man, Alex Aguilar. Yummy! How blessed are the woman of Carver to have this hot steamy guy to pine over every day.

Thank goodness we all have the same fourth period class. This means we all have the same lunch. Yay! Can you imagine what it would be like if we had separate lunches—it would be a social disaster.

By the time the bell rings for lunch, I'm famished. I left in such a hurry this morning, I didn't have a chance to grab anything to eat. I'm lucky I put money in my backpack or I'd have to chew my finger nails off for lunch—I guess that's better than eating my toenails. Ha ha! No, not really…any one of my friends would let me bum something from their lunch or would buy me something of my own.

Baked chips, salads, mini everything…this Healthy Kids crap sucks! What happened to the good ol' days of pizzas, cookies, and nachos? I guess I'll have to settle for a granola bar and water. I'll just stuff my face with whatever I can find when I get home. This nutritious food is not going to cut it. If only all those lazy fat *mo-fos* would just turn off their video games and go outside and run around a little, we wouldn't have to eat this cardboard crap they're trying to pass off as healthy. Okay, so I know I'm not skinny…just a little *big-boned*, but at least I exercise, sometimes.

I stop abruptly as we begin to walk away from the snack bar line.

"Where in the hell are we gonna sit?" I ask. There are students everywhere. They already have their spots. I get nervous all the sudden.

"Just keep walking. Act like we know where we're going," Amy says, as she leads the way.

"How about there, by the tree?" Keesh suggests.

I walk ahead. "Let's go for it. I don't want to walk in circles all lunch period," I say.

We find our spot—a small hill, with a shady tree, in the middle of a grassy area—in the quad. I open my granola bar and begin searching for Alex. I practically break my neck scanning every inch of the quad for a glimpse of his hotness. Much to my disappointment, I cannot find him anywhere. He must have a secret place or have first lunch. Oh…that would suck! Although, I'm sure I can find some other candidates to feed my boy crazy appetite. High school is like a buffet of cute guys.

Lunch doesn't last long before the bell rings and the masses start migrating to fifth period. All of us have P.E. next, then English. It's kind of cool that we have so many classes together. The only classes we don't share are first and second, they're flip-flopped though—Steph and I in one and Amy and Keesha in the other. It's to be expected, since we're all on the honors track. I think the four of us have basically had the same classes together since sixth grade. That's the way it works. All the smart kids are always grouped together. They wouldn't dare put us with the *regular* kids. Our parents would probably flip thinking we'd start doing all sorts of bad things from fraternizing with the riff raff. Little do they know, it's really the other way around—shhh, don't tell anyone though.

"So what'd you think of Ms. Gelson?" Keesha asks as we leave our sixth period class.

Amy speaks up first, "She seems alright, but seriously, do we have to start off the year with Shakespeare?"

"I was thinking the same thing! Isn't there an author that lived like in the last ten, even hundred years, that is worth reading." I roll my eyes. "I mean, it's like the whole world evolves except for in English. I think our parents, and grandparents, maybe even Jesus Himself read freakin' Shakespeare their freshmen year in high school." My voice gets higher and my face hotter as I complain. I *hate* Shakespeare.

Steph is waiting, on edge, to get a word in. "What the hell is the point in reading *Romeo and Juliet* in the first place? It's not like we all don't know the sad stupid story. What psycho girl would kill herself over a dumb guy anyways? Chicas..." We all look at Steph and she begins, "FRIENDS ARE FOREVER..."

"BOYS WHATEVER!" we all shout, putting our hands together to form a "W". We stop, look at each other again, and then laugh our asses off. Hey, it's silly...I know...but it's much better than what the guys say, "Bros Before Hos". This has been one of our favorite shout-outs since we were in middle school. That sounds funny, doesn't it, "since we were in middle school."

It's only our first day of high school and already junior high seems like so long ago.

4

Waiting two weeks for the first home football game seems like an eternity, but now the time is here. I get to see Alex in his football uniform—you know... the one with the tight pants that show off his muscular legs, firm bootie...and other *thrilling* shapes.

I can't wait!

Time is dragging as I begin to get ready. School has been out for about an hour and I'm going nuts with boredom killing time till I get to jet out of the house for the game. My parents wanted me to be home immediately after school—without any of my friends in tow—since I'm going to be out for most of the night. My friends' parents followed suit and they all had to spend "quality time" at home too.

What's the deal with that? I hate when parents think that way. We all know this ridiculous irrational mentality—"Since you are going out tomorrow night, you need to stay home with your family tonight." As if they're going to spend time with me contemplating the meaning of life, or reminiscing about the good old days. Yeah right! They just want to know that I'm here, in this house, with them, dreading the slow, lonely passing hours till I get to escape.

Okay, so it's not that bad—I've been known to exaggerate—but it would be so much better if my girls were here with me, or if I was with them. It pretty much sucks trying to figure out what I'm going to wear all by myself. Well, not really by myself—I think I've called Steph like five times, and Keesha has called me a couple times too and they have each talked to Amy.

What a process...

We do have part of our wardrobe already selected for us—these lame ASB shirts which Jen turned into some pretty hot tops by cutting slits down the sides and tying the pieces in knots to hold the shirt together—so it shouldn't be too difficult to complete the ensemble. But hey, it takes a lot out of you to figure out the right jeans and shoes to wear. I think I've tried on five pairs of jeans already—I know that sounds dumb, but seriously, they all fit a little different. And, how about these accessories? Earring, no earrings. Belt, or no belt. That is a task in itself. Not to mention my hair...what am I going to do with my *hair*? Do I wear it up, like athletic looking, since I'm going to a game? Or do I leave it down, flat-ironed, sleek, smooth, sexy?

"Sexy"...that's a laugh...like a 14 year-old can, or even should be *sexy*. But, I sure as hell am going to try—just without a thong, that's for sure.

Six o'clock...finally...I sprint out the door and head to school—I've been watching the minutes pass in slow motion on the kitchen clock for the last twelve minutes. I'm like Michael Phelps off the starting blocks at the sound of the gun, getting to school in world record time.

My legs don't even hurt, or I'm too excited to notice. Miraculously, I'm the last one here. How did this happen? I guess it's my lucky day—I don't have to wait like I usually do. Hopefully, I'll be as *lucky* for the rest of the night!

Before we enter the stadium, we find a secluded spot under a giant oak tree in the quad.

"So did you bring it?" Keesha asks, eyes wide-open and anxious.

"What do you think?" Amy snaps, revealing four mini-bar sized bottles of Malibu Rum from her backpack—you can't lug around a full bottle too easily, we've tried that before. And we can't drink beer—anyone can smell it a mile away. The scent of Malibu can easily be played off as any sweet-scented body spray.

My mouth starts to water as I look at the little palm trees on the side of the bottle. Ever since we got our first taste at Amy's eighth grade graduation party, we've been having a great time trying different drinks throughout the summer. Amy's parents have a well-stocked bar and never notice when something is missing. So far, the coconut-flavored rum is our favorite, and drink of choice.

"Do you really think we should do this?" Steph asks, worriedly. "It's only the first football game, and we actually have jobs to do tonight...don't you think Mr. Mitchell will notice?"

"Geez, Steph, you're such a buzz kill" I tease, rolling my eyes. "So what if it's the *first* football game? That's exactly why I wanna take a shot...you know, take the edge off, kill the nerves, loosen up." I wiggle around and take Steph's arms to shake her up a bit. "It's not like we're going to be falling all over the place with this wimpy excuse for a drink anyway," I joke, holding on to my miniature drink.

I crack the top open and down the few ounces of the thick, sweet, coconut concoction till it's all gone. I can feel a tiny bit of warmth go through my body from my throat, down to my stomach, and then to my toes. Just a little though...I'm not a *lightweight* or anything.

"Damn Meg, you could have waited for us," Amy whines, obviously irritated with me. Then she quickly pops open her own bottle and chugs it down within seconds.

She licks her lips, then speaks again. "We could have toasted to the...football team...or to *you* and *Alex*...and your hot, wild, sex on the fifty yard line," she jokes as she motions a fake toast at me. "You might get lucky tonight Meg. You look hot! You should straighten your hair more often."

Was that a compliment? From Amy?

Keesha is already closing her drink. She threw it back without me even noticing. But Steph is still holding her prize with disgust, like it's filled with Anthrax or something.

"Let's not let yours go to waste," I tell Steph as I snatch the bottle from her hand. I take a sip, then pass it to Amy and Keesha so they can finish it off.

"Someone has to watch out for your *drunk* asses," Steph groans with an attitude. She's the mommy of the group, always watching out for us. The rest of us can't say no to a good time. But Steph, she doesn't really like the feeling of not being completely in control. Steph just chills and takes it all in. Keesha, Amy, and I are a different story.

We toss the tiny bottles in a paper bag, wad it up, and ditch them in a trash can. This is *too* easy! If they only knew...our parents, our teachers, everyone...everyone who thinks that we are so different, so special.

We walk out of the darkness, noticing the stadium is already filled with people—students, parents, little kids, school staff, security. We head over to the handball courts where we're supposed to meet our class.

The football team is already on the field doing stretches. I can't tell one guy from another with their helmets on. They all look the same...and shit! I don't even know what number Alex is. What a freakin' loser I am. Seriously...that little piece of information would be useful. Ugh!

We join our classmates to get down to business. So the event—for ASB, anyways—goes like this: each class has to create a balloon arch in their class color. We also need to put up posters representing our class all over the home side of the stadium. At halftime, Mr. Mitchell is going to lead a spirit yell, or class yell. It's supposed to be a competition between the classes. We've already been told that freshmen don't have a chance. *Why not?* I think to myself, we can yell just as loud as everyone else.

We begin to blow up balloons full of helium. All the freshmen are looking at each other for help, but there's one big problem—none of us know how to make an arch full of balloons. It's not like we've taken Balloon Arch 101 before getting into this class. Shoot...come to think of it...it should be a prerequisite. None us know what the heck we're doing.

"No, I think you do it like this," one guy says, as he snags a tied balloon from another guy's hand.

"No, you loser, you do it like this," Amy yells, showing them how to tie the balloons together. I honestly don't know how to make it work, so I'm not going to try and fake it, which is what I think Amy is doing.

The twine is getting tangled and we seem to be doing a better job of tying each other up than creating anything that looks like an arch. And it has nothing to do with our pre-game beverages either—although Steph makes us promise to never drink before another ASB activity again.

"Hey, so whatcha guys working on. You look like you need help," this guy in a red shirt asks. He's definitely a senior.

We all stop to look at the upperclassman who's trying to talk to us. "We can't quite figure out how to get this arch put together," Steph admits.

"No prob, I can help. We had this problem too the first time we tried," Rusty says, with a smile. I remember him from the party. Who can forget a name like Rusty?

He instructs us to blow up the balloons and tie them together in a bunch of different ways. Blow the balloon, tie it off. Wrap the twine here on this balloon, then there on that balloon. Then do it all again. Before I realize it, we have about ten sets of balloons on this arch. It's really working.

Wait a minute. One cluster comes loose from the twine and sets off into the dark sky. Wait, another one escapes.

"What the heck is happening," I shout. "We're losing the balloons."

Rusty, the name should have been a clue, begins to laugh as one by one, the clusters of balloons fly away.

"Get the hell out of here, you jerk!" Keesh yells.

Steph watches Rusty as he walks away laughing. "This sucks. Our class is going to hate us."

"Who cares...let's just decorate a little, so we don't look so stupid," I suggest.

That is how we end up with a float full of ugly posters and balloon clusters, while the other ones look like they belong in the damn Thanksgiving Day Parade. Needless to say, we do not win the class yell. Once the freshmen in the bleachers got a look at us, they were probably too embarrassed to yell or cheer.

Ugh...LOSERS!

5

While the football game is a bust, not only for us but for the team who suffers a disastrous loss, the after party is going to be freakin' awesome—yup, I did say "*after party*"! Unlike many freshmen, we're actually invited. Our cool factor must have shot up in high school because as we strut our way from the stadium to the after party, we hear a honk and then a Volkswagen Golf pulls over.

Can it be?

"Wassup?" Alex asks, with his big brown eyes so hypnotic, my knees are about to buckle.

Crap, all he said is 'wassup' and I think I'm going to melt.

"Hey, Alex!" Amy shoots back, noticing I'm in a trance.

"What's up Alex?" Steph says.

She knows I'm in lust with Alex. It was weird to admit, at first, since he's going out with her sister. But she doesn't seem to care much. Lydia and Steph aren't very close and she says Lydia likes a new guy every day, even though she is with Alex right now.

"You wanna ride to the party?" the other guy asks. He is not as cute as Alex, but he's alright: spiky dark hair, nice smile, and a golden tan that brings out his piercing blue eyes. This guy was not at the end of the summer party. I would've remembered those blue eyes.

"Yeah, that'd be cool," I say in a strained voice trying to hide my excitement—and my nervousness, "but there's two of you …and four of us…you think we'll *fit*?"

Have you ever seen a Volkswagen *Golf*? Alex's car is like the size of a Hot Wheel. I'm surprised two big football players can even squeeze into that thing, much less four more girls, two of which are on the *big-boned* side.

But we fit, all six of us.

Just a short drive and we arrive at the party. The guys go along ahead of us. They are nice enough to give us a ride but apparently, they sure as hell don't want to be seen with freshmen. That's okay though, at least Alex cared enough to give us a ride, right? Maybe he saw us walking and thought, "there's my girl...she shouldn't be walking the streets at night by herself...I don't want her to get hurt or anything...I'll give her a ride...on my *lap!*" Okay, okay...so maybe I'm getting a little carried away, again!

But hey...he did give us a ride.

So who cares if we don't go in the party together.

The street is filled with cars, teenagers walking to and from the party, and the lights from the D.J. can be seen coming from the backyard as we get closer. The music isn't too loud. I can still make out the loud roar of kids and the sound of some of them actually puking their guts out in the bushes.

Goal for the evening: don't throw up!

"This doesn't look like such a good idea, after all," Steph cautions. She probably sees the girl dry heaving in the bushes. I was hoping she wouldn't notice that.

Or she witnesses, like I do, the half naked couple in the blue Honda Civic as we walk by. Damn, I wish I had those abs. I'd walk around naked everywhere if I had a body like that girl's. I doubt that chick gets *supersized* French fries with every meal—but I'm not about to give up that habit, even if my mom wants me to. Staying clothed is definitely worth it.

"Steph, don't even trip," Keesh snaps.

"Yeah, it will be fun," I say. "If it gets too crazy, we'll go, but let's, at least, check it out."

"Seriously, if you're still buggin' in about an hour, we'll bounce, okay?" Keesha lightens up a bit because she can tell Steph is worried.

Amy stands there acting pissy with her hands on her hips. She sighs as she tucks a piece of her long wavy hair behind her ear. I swear, if she rolls her eyes one more time, they're going to pop out of her beautifully made up head. And if they don't, I might have to do it for her. I hate her freakin' *attitude* sometimes. I mean, sure, we all have our moods, but Amy's affect all of us. It's like if she's not happy, no one is happy. When she gets all pissy like this, I try to stay calm, but one of these days...I'm gonna lose it.

I look at each of my friends and turn to head towards the party, "Geez, let's go already, I wanna see Alex!"

They follow and finally, we're all heading toward the party. Sometimes I think it would be better if we left Steph at home, since she worries so much. If she didn't trip over everything, then Amy wouldn't get so witchy. The tension makes everyone, especially me, feel uncomfortable. Every time we want to do something the least bit exciting, Steph hesitates and Amy gets pissy. I guess it's good that Steph's cautious, but sometimes it just...*bugs*!

The closer we get, the more intense the music is. Of course, Keesha and I have already started to feel the rhythm as we walk into the backyard. The latest hip-hop tunes are coming from the speakers, and multi-colored lights are circling the place. Strobe lights make people look like robots as they dance and move from here to there.

I can't wait to get on the dance floor. However, we come to a stop at the first empty place—a cement bench that sits stylishly in front of a flower bed. Corey's parents must've had their backyard professionally landscaped. Amy throws down her purse and takes a seat. Steph does the same. They look scared. *As if* we've never been to a party before.

"Let's dance," I say, nodding my head toward the dance floor.

Keesh is standing right next to me. "Let's hit it, girl," she says, with a little shake of her bootie.

"You guys coming?" I ask.

"Nah, I'm just gonna chill for now," Steph says.

Amy shakes her head and looks at us like we're stupid for even asking.

Keesh and I walk over to where people have crowded to dance. I don't care if I'm dancing with another girl, I'm not the only one doing this. Many of the guys seem to be more interested in tapping the kegs of beer. Keesha and I find our groove, the movements come naturally. I love the feeling of the music pulsing through my body. The music gets faster, my hands move through the air, my hips thrust, heat floods my body from head to toe. I hit every beat with every inch of my being. If only everything could make me feel as good as dancing.

We dance our way through about three songs before I catch a glimpse of Amy and Steph still sitting in the same spot as if their asses are nailed to the bench. I motion to Keesha that I'm leaving the dance floor, and she follows.

"Damn, girl, you were hittin' it out there," Keesha shouts over the music, with a giant smile on her face. She takes the hair tie from around her wrist and pulls her braids into a loose pony tail at the back of her head.

"Thanks! It's freakin' hot though," I say, breathlessly. I pull my damp sweaty hair off the back of my neck, hoping it will cool me down. "I haven't had that much fun in a long time. Let's check out Steph and Ames, they look bored."

Keesha stops suddenly.

"Not so fast Meggie, Amy looks like she is having a good time now." I can hear the sarcasm in Keesha's voice. "Just act normal though, don't flip out, okay?" She puts her hand on my arm.

The crowd clears my line of sight to Amy and Steph, and I see what Keesh is talking about. Alex is standing next to Amy—*close* to Amy—and they're talking. I hesitate before I go any further. I need time to think, time to soak this all in. Maybe they're so close because they can't hear each other over the music. Maybe he is asking about me, or she is talking me up to him. But, the more I see, the more I realize it doesn't look like that at all. Amy has her flirt face on in full force. I've seen it before, the intensity in her eyes, like a mountain lion ready to pounce. She smiles, licks her lips, raises an eyebrow, and whips her hair from her face with a subtle laugh.

What are they saying?

"I'm fine, Keesha," I say as I begin walking again. This time it feels like we're moving in slow motion. Everything else around me is a blur. "I'm good, let's check this shit out."

"Hey ladies." Alex's friend stops us dead in our tracks. "Wassup, I didn't think you made it in. I saw your other friends, but not you two. You diggin' your first high school party?"

"Uh...yeah," I mutter, trying to keep my eyes on Amy and Alex.

"Yeah, we were out their gettin' our swang on." Keesha saves me from looking like a dumb ass as usual. "You know, that music is sick! Do you dance?"

Alex's friend smiles. What the hell is his name?

"Hell yeah...especially after a few of these." He chuckles, holding up a sixteen ounce red plastic cup. Gee, I wonder what's in there. "Come on, let me hook you up."

Keesha nudges me to follow him. She shrugs her shoulders and smiles as if to say "it can't hurt."

I follow but am still distracted by what I'm leaving behind.

"So you wanna shot or a beer?" Alex's friend asks.

"Whichever line is shorter," I blurt out rather quickly.

"You're my kind of girl."

I can feel the blood rush to my cheeks. I probably look like a cherry tomato.

Keesha lets out a light giggle.

"Good to know," I shoot back. "Hey, what's your name? I don't think you ever told us and my mom says I'm not supposed to talk to strangers."

"Uh...so you can't talk to strangers but you can get in a *car* with them," he teases. "Now, that doesn't sound safe, does it?"

"Well, we didn't get in the car with only *you*—we know Alex!"

"Yeah, well, Alex is a little tied up over there, so I guess I'll have to do," he says, with a wink.

There is something about him. He's a little cute. Not, I wanna jump your bones right now sexy hot, but he is cute. And is he flirting? I thought I could be good at this. But I'm just a freshman and I'm totally flustered. I can't stop blushing. My face is hot and it's taking me forever to come up with something to say. What the hell is going on here? I look up at him. It's his eyes...the baby blues are just sucking me in.

"So freshmen, wanna hit the dance floor?" he asks.

"Why not!" Keesha slaps me on the back to wake me from my stupor. "Let's go Meggie!"

Alex's friend guides us to the dance floor, with a beer in one hand, and his other on the small of my back. Hmm...

Keesha looks all giddy, beaming like she is at Disneyland. Does she know something I don't?

We push our way into the crowds of bobbing heads and find a spot near the middle. It's a struggle, but I can occasionally catch a glimpse of Amy and Alex. He's leaning into Amy, talking into her ear, his nose nuzzled in her hair. She looks down smiling, her hand brushes up against his lower arm.

What the hell is going on?

Am I overreacting? I don't think so.

They look like a *couple* standing there chatting so cozy. Where is Lydia? Amy is pretty bold to be so close to her man— she can't be too far away. And Steph is right there too. How can she act like this right in front of Steph? Sure, I want to be Amy right now, but I would never make it so obvious. The guy has a girlfriend for crying out loud!

Oh my gosh! If Lydia doesn't get to her first, I'm going to kill her!

I gulp a full breath of air. I actually think I forgot to breathe for a minute here.

My face must look distressed because his friend asks me what's wrong.

"Uh...nothing," I lie. "This is a whack song...just waiting for it to change."

"B.J." He grins.

"*Excuse me!*" I respond angrily to what I think is a question.

"No, not *that*." He laughs. "My *name* is B.J.! I wasn't propositioning—you've got a dirty mind, little one."

Keesha can't stop laughing—at my expense, of course. Can my face get any more red? I want to be invisible. I can't believe I thought he was asking me something about...you know! Kill me *now*!

"My bad," I barely let out.

"Well, if you're *interested*." B.J. winks.

"Don't *even* think about it," I shoot back, with a snap in my neck. This guy is starting to grow on me.

"Wassup girls!" Jen yells, joining us. She starts dancing and then shouts, "Dang, looks like my sister isn't wasting any time with Alex. Shit, he just broke up with Lydia after school and she's already got her claws in him!"

What? Wait a minute! Did I just hear this correctly? Alex and Lydia broke up? Amy is not wasting time? Amy has her claws in him? Wait! This is *not* happening!

"Jen, you're so freakin' drunk, you don't know what the hell you're talking about," I snap at her.

"Yeah, Amy doesn't like Alex!" Keesha yells over the music.

"Well, Alex likes her," B.J. interrupts. "He's been feelin' her since we saw you guys at orientation. The guy's been spittin' game all night. That's why he got rid of Lydia...but you didn't hear that from me."

I think I'm going to faint. The room...no, the sky is spinning. I cannot believe it. I cannot freakin' believe it. How can she do this to me? Amy knows how much I like Alex. When I get a hold of her, I swear I'm going to...I'm gonna...ugh! I can't even think of something.

Breathe, breathe, I tell myself.

Keesha, sensing trouble, grabs my hand, and before I know it, we're in the front yard.

"Look, we don't know what's going on, so *calm* down!"

My face is burning and I can feel the tears in my eyes. I look up into the sky, willing myself not to let them fall. I take deep breaths and suck them back in. I'm not going to cry over a guy who obviously doesn't know I exist. But I'm hurt, definitely hurt, by my so-called friend. Earlier, she was talking about toasting to me and Alex, and our crazy sex on the fifty yard line. Now it looks like she's got the ball and she's gonna do him on the fifty yard line, *and* in the end zones. Ugh! It's not like she doesn't know how I feel about him. What kind of friend talks to a guy she knows you have feelings for? Who does that?

I take a few minutes to make sure my eyes stay dry before I speak, "Thanks Keesh, I'm all good...seriously...let's go dance."

"Hey, there you are..." Steph shouts. "Meg, we need to talk. I gotta tell you something!"

"It's okay Steph," I half-smile and lie. "Jen told us already. I'm good, but how's Lydia?"

"Oh." Steph sounds surprised. "Lydia is so gone. I guess you could say she's drinking her pain away. She probably could've cared less anyway, you know how she is. She'll be all hugged up with someone else by the end of the night." We all look at each other and nod. We know Lydia.

Steph continues, "She's so freakin' wasted right now, it's embarrassing. Everyone else thinks she's the life of the party. The last time I saw her, she was dancing on a table. I tried to get her to come down—she chugged some more and told me to eff-off. I can't even find her now. Oh well, I tried...she's gonna be in trouble later!"

"Oh shit, your parents are gonna kill her!" Keesha laughs.

"We're gonna go dance, wanna come?" I suggest, needing to take my mind off of Amy and Alex—ugh, their names together make me want to puke, or *cry*.

"Let's do this!" Steph shouts as we make our way back to the party. It's about time she loosens up—its only taken her half the freakin' night.

We're dancing, hands in the air, feeling the bass pumping from the speakers like a heartbeat. We're just goofing around. Steph goes old school with the cabbage patch. I start doing booty bumps with Keesh. Steph puts her hands up and we both slap her hands.

"Hey, I brought you guys a little sumtin', sumtin'," B.J.'s voice comes through the crowd.

I see the shot glasses in his hand and say, "Cool," as I take one.

"Oh, hey!" He gestures at Steph. "You can have mine."

"No thank you," Steph responds. "It's not my thing, so knock yourself out." She pushes the shot away from her.

Keesha takes one for herself, we clink glasses, and toss them back.

Wow—that is hot! Superhot! I should've asked what it was before I drank it. It sure as hell wasn't tequila, not that tequila would've been much better. Remind me to never drink *this* again! Ugh!

Keesha must be thinking the same thing. "What the hell was that?" she demands.

"*Aftershock*, you've never tried it before? Oh...I keep forgetting...you're just *freshmen*," B.J. taunts.

"What the hell is *that* supposed to mean?" I scoff. "What, because you're a *senior*, you've sampled every kind of drink there is."

"Easy killer...I was joking."

He wraps his free hand around my waist and pulls me closer to him. He seems to be dancing with me, only. Keesha and Steph dance together and when his back is turned, they're all smiles

and giving me the thumbs up. Okay, B.J. is getting cuter by the minute—Alex who? Yeah right…as if I can forget about him.

"Where have you guys been?" Amy shouts, pushing her way through the crowd toward us. "I've been looking all over the place for you."

She avoids looking at me, directing her questions to Steph and Keesha.

"We've been dancing right here the whole time," Keesha says, coldly. "I guess you weren't looking too hard, huh. What have you been doing…besides looking for us?"

Amy probably senses the attitude in her voice because she ignores Keesha's question.

"Are you guys ready to go yet? Alex said he'd give us a ride to Steph's house."

How cute? We're all going to get in the car with Amy and Alex—they better keep the PDA to a minimum or I'm going to poke Amy's eyes out with her fake claws.

"Sounds good," B.J. announces. "I'll go with."

We all change direction to make our way out of the party. B.J. guides me with his hand on my back again. Hmm, interesting.

The ride home is quiet. I sure as hell don't know what to say. I hate confrontations. Keesh and Steph keep looking at me as if I'm going to flip out or something.

When we get to Steph's house—her parents aren't going to be home until late so we all made arrangements to stay the night there—Alex and B.J. get out of the car to let us out on both sides. Alex catches Amy's hand, pulls her toward him, and kisses her—yes, I said he kisses her. That was supposed to be my kiss. That is supposed to be me! She doesn't even shy away from him. It's like they've done this a million times. Can I say…*bitch*?

We all turn away quickly—and again Keesh and Steph are watching me, waiting for my reaction.

"Hey Megan," B.J. startles me.

"Yeah," I screech. I can feel a lump in my throat.

"Can I get your digits?" he asks with a grin.

"Oh...uh...sure...I guess," I say, confused. Can I sound any more stupid?

"Well, you don't *have* to...I just thought it would be cool to talk to you some more."

"Oh, sure...you just caught me off guard...I'd like to talk to you again too."

We exchange numbers, he gives me a hug—a *hug*, not a *kiss*—and they leave.

6

We're all asleep in the living room when Steph's parents come in.

"Stephanie, wake up right now!" Steph's dad says, sternly.

"What...what...what happened?" Steph moans, in a daze.

"Where in the hell is Lydia? She is not in her room. Did you see her tonight?"

Steph sits up and the rest of us stay quiet. I don't know if the other girls heard him, but he sure as heck startled me out of my sleep. "Uh...yeah...we all went to the same party after the game...but she was with her friends and I was with mine. It's not like we went together."

I can tell Steph is trying to leave out the details.

"Where in the hell was this party?" he questions her.

"It was over on Cypress Street."

"Get your butt up and put some shoes on...you're going to take me there."

"What? No way Dad, why don't you call her or some of her friends? You're going to make me look like an idiot," Steph cries.

"Don't you think I tried that already? Let's go, I want to check this out before I have to call the police."

Steph looks at us embarrassed, and angry. Everyone is definitely up now.

They leave in a hurry and I can't get back to sleep. Where could Lydia be? It's already five in the morning. I rustle around in my blankets, trying to relax. But I'm awake now.

Amy is the first to break the silence.

"Hey Meg...are you mad at me?" Amy whispers.

We didn't even talk when we came in last night. Everyone got their pjs on and went to bed. Normally, we would stay up all night talking and laughing about who said what and who did what at the party. I know Keesh wanted to say something, but I asked her not to. I wasn't sure what I was thinking yet, or what I wanted to say. I think I was afraid to say anything, so we just went to sleep.

"Last night I was...I wanted to rip your hair out...but now, I'm not angry. I'm more sad and disappointed, I guess."

I don't look at her. I stare at the ceiling, all bundled up in my blankets, fixated on the faint signs of brush strokes from the last time Steph's parents painted. I'm sure Keesha is dying, trying to keep her mouth shut. She is a sweet person, but if any of us are hurting, she is there to defend, to the death, like a mother bear protecting her cubs.

"You know, it's not like I went after him. I didn't even know he broke up with Lydia. He came to me. He said that since the day of Freshmen Orientation, he couldn't stop thinking of me..."

"Damn, Amy...would you just shut the hell up!" Keesh interrupts, fiercely. "You just have to rub it in, don't you?"

"I'm not trying to rub it in...I'm just telling Meg what happened. He was so nice and I can't believe he feels this way about me. I figured since he didn't have feelings for her, she wouldn't mind if I took a shot with him."

Un-freakin'-believable!

"*Seriously*! You don't even like him!" I shout, angrily.

"Well, I didn't...but you never know what'll happen. I think I like him, *now*."

Keesha shoots in, "You *think* you like him. So, because you *think* you like him, you don't mind stabbing one of your best friends in the back. You are such a *bit*..."

Amy doesn't let her finish but we all know what she was going to say. "Wait a minute, I didn't stab her in the back. It's not like I stole him away. She never even had him. Really Meg, you've only talked to him, nothing else. The only one that should be remotely pissed at me is Lydia. But she was so wasted last night, she probably doesn't even know what happened yet."

"You're right, Amy. He *was* never mine. And sure, I've only really talked to him, but isn't that how it's supposed to start? You knew I had feelings for him. That should count for something. But oh well...hope you guys live happily ever after," I concede.

"Wow, really...thanks Meg, I knew you would be okay with this," Amy gushes, not even recognizing my sarcasm.

"*Karma*," I state, gritting my teeth.

"What?" Amy asks, confused.

"Karma...you know, what comes around goes around...you'll see."

Or at least, I hope she will.

We hear voices and Steph comes in.

"Did you find her?" Keesha sits up to ask.

"Yeah, we sure did," Steph snickers.

"Where was she?" I ask, sitting up as well.

"In the bushes," she laughs.

"What?" I'm confused. "Where?"

"At the party...you know how Corey's house has those massive bushes all the way around his yard?" We nod. "Well, we found her passed out in the bushes—freakin' lush!"

I put my hands to my mouth, "Oh my God!"

"Seriously?" Keesha says, surprised but amused.

"Seriously!" Steph is in tears from laughing. "She is so busted! We won't be seeing her at any parties any time soon."

7

I can't believe I even rolled my ass out of bed to go to school this morning. Even though I'm on my way to first period, I actually contemplated staying home. The thought of dealing with Amy makes my head hurt.

All these visions keep popping up in my mind, like a slide show repeating over and over again. First, it's an image of Amy and Alex kissing when we got out of the car Friday night. It plays in slow motion for a more terrorizing effect. Then, Amy says over and over, like a scratched CD, that Alex doesn't like me. Each time I hear the words, it's like another stab through my heart, like she's pushing pins through a voodoo doll. My favorite, and most torturous, is the mental picture of Amy and Alex holding hands. As they walk passed me, Alex pats me on the head like I'm just a little kid—or worse, a little sister. That last scene hasn't happened, and I hope it never will. I need to do something to stop this constant replay of painful images.

Steph is already standing outside our classroom waiting. I'm tired and not in the mood for the talking head—I swear if Mrs. Caldwell gives us one more worksheet, I'm going to scream. Did anyone inform her this is an honors class? Does she know we're capable of more than just filling in the blanks? Seriously, how can a teacher manage to take something as complex and exciting as the Earth, the one thing in the universe that can sustain life, for better or worse, and turn it into the single most boring thing known to man? I can actually feel the life being sucked from my pores as I get closer to the door.

When Keesha shows up and suggests an alternate plan, I'm oh so eager to concede.

"You two are not seriously considering *ditching* class? We're honors students for cryin' out loud, we're not...*regular* kids!" Steph says with disgust, turning to gesture to some of the students walking by.

"Why not? My brain cells die off exponentially every minute I'm forced to sit through another one of Mrs. C's stupid lectures," I say, trying to convince myself ditching class isn't as bad as it sounds. "You know, we should probably be teaching the class for her. It's a joke!"

Just because Mrs. Caldwell has been a teacher for like twenty years doesn't mean she should be allowed to teach honors. Seriously, with her lack of teaching, we'll never be prepared for biology next year.

"Steph, you don't have to come," Keesha adds. "You can actually give us the stupid handouts later." She looks at me. "Better yet, Meggie, we can create our own and show her what *good* notes actually look like."

"Sounds good...but...are you sure no one *else* is coming?" I ask, hopeful we'll be going alone.

"No...no one *else* is coming...you think I would tell Amy about this after Friday night? Besides I saw her with Alex and his crew this morning. I know she saw me and she just looked away...so, screw her! Looks like it's just you and me, huh."

"Okay...whatever...the bell is going to ring soon so let's get outta here," I proclaim.

"You guys...be careful! Wait, when are you gonna come back?" Steph asks, worriedly.

"We'll be back before lunch...don't trip, Steph...we wouldn't make you eat lunch by yourself," Keesha says, comforting our friend.

"Okay...late," Steph says, as she heads into class.

We make our way off the school grounds. Adrenaline begins to rush as we cross the street. My heart is beating like I've just had twenty blended coffee drinks topped with whip cream. Then, fear begins to strike as I realize I have no idea where we're going, and at the thought of getting caught. My parents will kill me if they find out. They would be devastated if they found out I did anything remotely wrong. I'm their sweet, innocent little girl—psshh...I begin to chuckle inside. The thought of me being sweet and innocent is definitely funny. My parents obviously have a distorted view of their daughter.

I guess I should just chill and enjoy myself. What's done is done, right?

I sure as hell have done a lot worse.

"So...where are we going?" I ask Keesh.

"You hungry?"

"Ha ha...that's a dumb question." I laugh.

"True. Let's go to the *Steel Grill*. Biscuits and gravy sound good right now." Keesha licks her lips and smacks them together.

"That does sound good! Hey...don't you think we look a little obvious right now...like we look like ditchers. I mean we have our backpacks and everything." I feel like every car that passes by is an undercover cop, like everybody is staring at us. I'm definitely paranoid.

"Well, I'm sure we look like we're ditching 'cause we are...but we could ditch the backpacks too," Keesha suggests. "Maybe we won't draw so much attention."

"Uh...and where would you suggest we dump these suckers?" I asks, shaking my bag.

"Here." She says, throwing her backpack into some bushes near an old people's home.

"No freakin' way!"

I have a bad feeling about this.

"Who's gonna look in the bushes on the off chance they might find a backpack full of class notes and an algebra two book?" Keesha says, sarcastically.

"Whatever...let's just go," I say, rolling my eyes and tossing my backpack beside hers in the brush. "It *better* be here when we get back."

I'm such a push-over, especially for biscuits and gravy!

We get a table at the Steel Grill and I'm surprised to see that we're only two of many students who appear to be missing first period. We've managed to find the hangout for morning ditchers. Actually, this is one of the few places within walking distance—there aren't a lot of options when you don't have a car, or a license.

A waitress comes by to take our drink orders and gives us place settings. We order our food too, biscuits and gravy with hash browns. The Steel Grill is definitely not a four-star restaurant—maybe a one-star, if they're lucky. The hard plastic cups are worn with actual bite marks around the rim. Seriously, I'm not exaggerating this time. The silverware looks polka dotted with water spots. At least, this time there isn't any leftover food crusted on them. The last time I was here I had to ask for a different fork twice before I got a semi-clean one.

"So did he call?" Keesha asks. I was wondering when this was going to come up.

We hadn't really talked since Saturday afternoon when we left Steph's house. Amy was probably too embarrassed to call any of us. It was either that, or she didn't want to hear any of the crap we were likely to dish out. Keesha and I kept missing each other. Steph is on somewhat of a lockdown. Since Lydia is in trouble, it kinda trickles down to Steph too. That sucks because she's the good one—out of all of us.

"Uh...who?" I hesitate. I know who she's asking about, but I don't know where to begin.

"Don't be stupid," Keesh snaps. "You *know* who I'm talking about. So what'd he say?"

"Alex or Ben?" I throw that out there, knowing this will make her wild with questions.

Keesha's eye widen, confused, yet intrigued. "Wait...Alex called you...and who is Ben?"

"Yeah, Alex called," I begin. "And B.J. is Ben."

"Speak to me, please. Make me understand 'cause I may have a 4.0, but I don't get what the hell you're talking about!"

"You want Alex or Ben first?"

"Uh…Alex," Keesha says, as she digs in to eat her food. When you order biscuits and gravy, your order comes super fast. They probably have a barrel of gravy in that kitchen.

"So, Alex called yesterday. I was surprised. He didn't even have my number, but guess who gave it to him?"

I take a bite, enjoying the creaminess of the gravy…and the biscuits, you can never go wrong with bread.

"Amy or B.J., Ben, whatever?" she replies, quickly. I can tell she is anxious to hear the juicy details.

I hurry to swallow my food and continue, "Amy…she was upset 'cause she felt like all of us were being mean to her. She thought we were going to gang up on her or something. Alex asked her what was wrong and she freakin' told him I liked him and I was pissed at her 'cause they hooked up…"

"She told him that…she's such a…blahhhh sometimes," Keesh grunts.

"So yeah…she is 'cause I felt like such a dumb ass. I didn't know what to say. I can't even believe he called to talk to me about it." I cringe, still embarrassed by the conversation I had with Alex. I stab a piece of biscuit with my fork and shove it into my mouth.

"So, what did he say?"

Keesha waits while I chew slowly, dragging out the suspense.

"He said he was sorry he didn't feel that way for me. He said he didn't know I felt that way about him."

"Yeah, yeah, yeah…what else?" Keesh motions quickly with her hands, as if to say "give me more."

"Anyway, he said he thought I was really funny that night at the party and he liked talking to me. He said I'm way too nice for him and that he's not good enough for someone like me…which was nice…I guess…but what does that say for Amy?"

"That she is a backstabbing *beeyotch* of a friend, so it doesn't matter if she gets with this ass who is probably gonna screw her over anyway."

"Wow...that was harsh!" I say, surprised. Keesh blurted that out like she had practiced it for days. "Anyway, he said he wants to be friends and hopes that he can still talk to me without leading me on...he said I seem like a fun person to be around, so I told him okay." I stab at another biscuit and hold it up. "It's all gravy."

"You're such a goof, Meggie. So...you're still going to talk to him...are you sure that's a good idea?"

"Why not?" I shrug. "That's what I liked about him in the first place—was that he was fun to talk to—maybe he's just better off as a friend than a boyfriend. I mean, look, he was nice enough to call. Most guys would've been like 'whatever', but he called."

I smile thinking about being friends with Alex.

"Hmm...if you're sure, but he better not hurt you or I'm gonna kick his cute ass...you know that don't you?"

"Yes, I do Keesh...thanks mommy!" I giggle. "You know...it wasn't too bad talking to him...kind of nice, really...like talking to you or Steph. I felt like I'd talked to him a million times before. I just wonder what's going to happen with him and Amy."

"Yeah...I wonder what she's gonna be like at lunch today." Keesha nibbles on the inside of her cheek while she takes a moment to think. "You think she'll sit with him or us?"

I pause, picturing more PDA between Amy and Alex during lunch. My stomach turns sour just thinking about it.

"I guess we'll see later."

"Wait a minute!" Keesha jumps in. "Tell me about B.J., or Ben...whatever his name is."

Oh yeah...at least this story will take my mind off of that last thought long enough for me to hold down my breakfast.

"So that's his real name," I begin. "I guess his freshman year on football, there were two Bens, the other was a senior. So he got nicknamed Ben Junior, and the guys ended up calling him B.J.

for short. It just stuck and I think since they're a bunch of pervs, they like the name B.J. for other reasons too...you get me?"

Keesha smirks, "I get it...I'm sure they love calling one of their boys *B.J.*."

"So anyways, he said the guys are really the only ones who call him that, so I can call him Ben or B.J., it doesn't matter."

"Well, that must've been a hard choice," she chuckles.

"Yeah...no kidding. Can you imagine my mom—Meg, there's a *B.J.* on the phone!" I say, imitating my mom's shrill voice.

We both laugh hysterically. My mom is so oblivious to things like that sometimes, she probably wouldn't even realize what she was saying.

Keesh snorts causing us both to go into hysterics. She keeps snorting, and it's like we can't stop. It's not even funny anymore, but we can't stop laughing. I manage to take a sip of my drink to try and calm myself.

"Okay, okay, okay, I'm good. I'm done," I say, wiping my eyes with a napkin. I take a deep breath so I can tame another outburst.

"Okay, no more laughing. Anyway, so what did you talk about?" she asks, still giggling.

"Just random stuff...nothing in particular. But we were on the phone for, like, almost two hours."

Keesha laughs, "Crap...is he gay?"

"What...just because a guy talked to me for more than fifteen minutes, he's gotta be gay?"

"Hey...I was just kidding...but seriously, is he?" Keesha asks, seriously this time.

"No stupid...he's not gay—just nice, I guess."

"So that was it, you just talked about nothing?"

"Well, he knew that I liked Alex...but he just talked like it was no big thing. I didn't even feel dumb," I reply.

"Hmm...this could get interesting," Keesha says, raising her brows up and down.

"Dang, we've been here forever," I say, as I look at the time. I pause to take the last couple bites of my breakfast. "Should we go?"

It always takes us forever to get through a meal. We talk too much—our food is usually cold before we finish it.

"I guess...if we leave now, we can make it back in time for third," Keesh answers.

Keesha and I get up from our booth, and head over to the counter to pay. There are still some students here, but most have already left.

8

I feel much better when we begin walking back to school. I'm over the fear. It's just like walking to school in the morning, no big deal. My heart is beating normal, it isn't racing like it was earlier.

Until…

"How sick…look at these tampons all tossed around, up and down the sidewalk," I comment on the periscope-looking plastic applicators and cotton corks that are scattered. "Hey do you remember when Amy's sisters were playing with her tampons and pads?"

A while back, Amy's little sisters got into a box of tampons from under the sink in the bathroom. They unwrapped them all and were pretending to be pirates looking for a buried treasure, peering through the applicator pushing it in and out. They also got into the sanitary pads, took the paper strips off the backs, and stuck them to different places around the house—X marks the spot is where the treasure was found. The treasure was the dynamite—or the cotton wads from the tampons. This story makes me smile every time I think about it.

"Yeah, I do. That was so funny. I thought Amy's mom was going to die." Keesh chuckles. She side-steps to avoid stepping on one of them. "At least they're not *used*."

"Sick!" I snap.

"Wa…Wait a minute…," Keesha says, as she notices sheets of paper whisping away over lawns and into the street.

"Oh shit…our bags!" I cry.

"Damn!" Keesha exclaims. She starts to jog over to the bush. I guess our secret hiding place wasn't much of a secret.

As we get closer, I stumble upon one of my folders, some Spanish notes, headphones, and a few highlighters. All my crap is spread out all over the place. I guess the bush did not do a good job of hiding our stuff. That bush is fired!

We gather our things and stuff what's left back into our bags. I'm only missing a calculator and my fake iPod—my cheap non-brand name MP3 player. Keesha is now heading back to school tamponless and without an algebra two book. So there *is* someone out there who wants to study the quadratic equation.

Karma.

There is that word again. This is what we get for ditching— our crap dumped out all over the street. I bet whoever found it was disappointed to find we're losers without drugs, money, or even condoms. My money was with me. I don't do drugs. And I don't need any condoms, not yet anyway.

"¿Señorita Miller, como se dice *pencil* en español?" Mrs. O'Brien is apparently asking me.

I'm not paying attention. I'm barely catching my breath from running up the stairs to be in my seat on time. I don't want to get detention for being tardy.

"Un lapis," Amy answers for me.

Is she being nice...trying to help me out? Or is she being a witch, trying to make me look bad?

"Gracias, Señora Chapman, pero la proxima vez espere su turno," she says, sternly.

Amy's face turns slightly pink. She's not used to teachers correcting her answers or her behavior. She's usually treated like a freakin' goddess in class.

Spanish goes by fast—reviewing basic words and simple phrases that can be used regularly in school. It's a good thing I don't need my notes. The work is really easy, but it's embarrassing to speak aloud.

Steph is the most embarrassed of all of us. Since she's Mexican, I mean...American of Mexican descent, she is expected to know Spanish—and she's supposed to be able to speak it with an accent. However, Steph's Spanish is about as good as ours. She is like fiftieth generation born here, she knows the *American* language—no accent necessary.

Fourth period *already*? Wow, I can get used to this skipping class thing. It's so easy—it can definitely become a habit, if it weren't for the loads of work I'd miss.

ASB begins like usual—utter chaos!

Students file in little by little, some grabbing lunch first before heading in. Since first lunch starts at the same time, some students opt to eat during class. It's not like they're going to get into trouble. It's like we have free rein to do whatever we want—well maybe not us freshmen, but the seniors can definitely do whatever the hell they please.

Mr. Mitchell rings his *own* bell about fifteen minutes into the period. Everyone gathers into the classroom and waits for their name to be called. Mr. Mitchell always calls roll, every day at the same time. If you're not here when he calls your name, you're marked absent. I'm always here so it doesn't matter much to me. I catch on really quick though. Once he calls roll, students just come and go as they please, and some actually leave and never came back.

Before excusing everyone, the next project is announced— rally committee will begin working on the Homecoming Rally and the activities committee must get started with the dance. Like always, Steph and Amy part ways with me and Keesh, to meet up with our committees. All the details for the dance are pretty much complete. The place where the dance is held takes care of everything. So our committee chair just asks for volunteers to sell tickets at lunch. The upperclassmen fill the slots before Keesh and I have a chance to even raise our hands.

The lunch bell rings and we're the first in line for our *healthy* snack. Another perk of being in ASB—we can get in line before the bell rings so we always have our lunch before other students can even make it out of their classrooms.

The four of us sit under our tree and begin to eat quietly. I think about what Keesha said this morning. Will Amy sit with us or is she going to ditch us for Alex and the football team? I have a feeling Steph and Keesha are thinking the same thing.

It isn't long before Amy whips out her brand new cell and touches the screen. She smiles, her cheeks flush as she reads the text. She gathers her stuff quickly, fumbling over her food and trying to get her stuff inside her bag. I know where she is going. We all know where she is going.

"Hey guys…I'll be back in a bit," she mutters. "I'm gonna go chill with Alex for a while."

"Have fun," I manage to say with a fake smile.

"Don't hurry on our account," Keesh says, sarcastically.

Steph doesn't say anything. She just smiles. Although, it looks about as sincere as mine is.

"Okay, bye," Amy mumbles as she walks away.

This is it.

Our tight-knit, real-life *Sisterhood of the Traveling Pants*— well, without the pants, or the travel—is coming to an end. This is just the beginning. I can feel it. We're not the same girls that were inseparable only just a few weeks ago. It's all changing now—just one guy, okay one freakin' hot guy, can do so much damage. What happened to "friends are forever, boys whatever?" Even though Amy is with the guy of my dreams, I don't want us to…just…fall apart.

We're supposed to be *forever*!

9

I can't believe soccer try-outs are Monday. It's only been a little over a month since school started and the thought of running for hours after school during practice seems daunting but my fat ass can use the exercise. This *Healthy Kids* crap is not helping any either, I just get home from school starving, and binge with some Skinny Cow ice creams—because one is not enough—and a diet soda. My mom is going to have to do some grocery shopping. Carrots and fat-free yogurt is not going to cut it once practice starts. French fries! I'm going to need some French fries.

Both Keesha and I are going to try out—she'll probably make Varsity and I might be lucky enough to make the Freshmen team. I love to play sports but I'm just not naturally athletic, especially with soccer. Keesh is good though. She's like the players in the World Cup—that freakin' good, really. She can do all kinds of tricks and stuff. I'm lucky if I don't trip while I'm dribbling the ball. My dad actually laughs at me, really, he laughs at me. The few times he's been to my games, he joked that he didn't want to tell anyone I was his daughter. Funny, but sad.

Seriously...I'm really not that bad. One time I even made a goal—it wasn't intentional or anything, but it was still a goal. Keesha was taking a corner kick and I was standing in my spot in the goal. Before I knew it the ball hit me in the *vajayjay*—you know, down there—and flew in the goal. I didn't even realize what happened until everyone starting screaming and running toward me to hug and congratulate me. Who cares if I didn't even mean for it to happen? It was still a goal, my goal!

I wish Steph would try out with us. It's not like you have to be MLS material to be on the Freshmen team—at least, we could be there together. She's the only one of us who isn't going to have something to do once soccer starts. Amy is never free now that she and Alex spend every freakin' waking moment together. She still hangs with us, but she has also started mingling with the senior girls as well. This would've probably happened anyway because her older sister Jen is a senior, but since she's with Alex now, it only makes it that much easier for her to ditch us at lunch or after school.

Not all the female seniors enjoy Amy's company though. The stereotypical hot, stuck-up cheerleaders hate her with a passion, since they have this prehistoric idea that the football players belong to them. The football team kind of sucks, so I would say they can have them, but this is Alex we're talking about. I guess if I can't have Alex, I'm secretly happy the stupid rah-rahs can't have him either, even though Amy will probably be one of them someday anyway. Actually, I'd be much happier if he hadn't chosen to be with one of my best friends.

It really bites how things have changed. Amy doesn't walk home with us anymore; she goes to the library for tutoring, even though she doesn't need it, so Alex can give her a ride home after his football practice. How ridiculous is that? Who wants to hang out in the library for two hours after school? By the time she gets home, the rest of us have already debriefed the day, eaten to our hearts content, finished our homework, checked out reruns of *The Hills*, and been on *MySpace* a *kabillion* times. What a waste of time for Amy? Damn, I guess Alex must be worth it. Actually, I know he's worth it and I wish I knew how *worth it* he really is.

There go my hormones again!

You would think I'm some middle aged woman hitting her stride or something, with the heat I feel down there just thinking about Alex's *worthiness*. The only thing I've ever done with a guy is kiss, and a little boob action. There were times when my hands, or the guys, were straying toward the nether regions but we either chickened out or got interrupted.

Maybe I'm all hot like this because I haven't kissed a guy since the eighth grade dance. It was a good one too. Eric is so freakin' hot—he must've watched soap operas or *Sex in the City* to know how to move his lips and where to put his hands. He always touched the side of my cheek first, then put his hand through my hair and pulled me toward him. It always started out gentle and sweet, then ended savage-like as I could feel the tug on my hair, and my lips and tongue molded into his. It didn't hurt or anything, it was roughly satisfying. I could live with kisses like that for the rest of my life. Let's just say I could've probably used a panty liner every time Eric kissed me. And he was a good boyfriend too. Why did I break up with him again?

Damn, maybe I forgot about Eric too soon? Hmm...I'm going to have to check him out in English on Monday. Since we have English sixth period, if things go well, I can talk to him after school too. Maybe a little hook-up will take my mind off Alex, and Amy.

And Ben too...what the hell is going on with him anyway?

I must've been daydreaming for quite a long time, because when Amy comes into my room, I realize I missed the whole movie. I remember watching the beginning and that's about it. I probably wouldn't have noticed the credits rolling if Amy hadn't shown up.

What the heck is *she* doing here?

"So what's up Amy?" Keesha glares at her. "Your calendar wasn't all booked up this weekend?"

Keesha can be rude sometimes, but Amy deserves it. I can't remember the last weekend we were all together. Oh wait...yes I can...it was when Alex and Amy hooked up for the first time. Wow...that seems like eons ago.

Amy just plops on my bed next to Steph. "So what are you guys doin' tonight?" she asks, acting as if nothing has changed.

"This is it," I say, throwing my hands into the air. "Don't faint or anything with all this excitement, okay."

I'm trying to be funny to break the ice, but I don't think it's working. They all just stare at me.

"Yeah, we're just going to hang out, watch movies, eat, that's about it." Steph gives her the run-down.

"Sounds good," Amy mutters. She then asks, hesitantly, "Mind if I stay?"

Keesh, Steph, and I look at each other surprised, before Keesha utters, "Go for it, knock yourself out."

We all just look at each other again, unsure what we're going to do or say next. I take out my storage totes with nail polish, files, clippers, all the mani-pedi essentials. I begin by swabbing away the polish from my toes, smearing black paint on my skin. The others begin pillaging through the boxes too. Keesha takes out some cotton balls to use with the nail polish remover. Amy takes out some bright blue nail polish. Steph grabs a nail file before walking over to my stereo.

Soon, all I hear is the familiar set of *America's Top 40* coming from my stereo. I love listening to *KIIS* at night. JoJo is freakin' hilarious.

"Girls, listen, listen...JoJo is going to do the Question of the Night!" I exclaim.

We all stop what we're doing and listen.

"Tonight, we're taking callers from people with the most embarrassing doctor's visit. We want to hear it all. What did you do? What did your doctor do? Who was it embarrassing for? Your doctor or for you? Let's take our first caller...we've got Kim here, calling in from the I.E....tell us your story," he announces.

"Hi JoJo...well, this one time I was in the patient room waiting for my doctor to come in. When he did, he had a big fat chub showing through his scrubs. I could actually see the shape of his friend in clear detail, I could probably pick it out in a line up," the caller says.

Oh my gosh! I would've died.

"Damn girl, what were you being seen for?" Jojo jokes.

"Only a cold, but I wonder who he saw before me." She chuckles.

"That's hilarious," Steph says, as she laughs. Amy and Keesh are laughing too, and nodding their heads.

"That was a good one." I continue to chuckle. We all go back to our nails, pausing every time JoJo comes on with another story.

"Hey...have you guys ever seen JoJo?" Steph asks.

"Oh my gosh, yes!" Amy replies, with excitement.

"He is so freakin' hot!" Keesh says.

"Totally...I wonder how old he is...he looks so young...too bad he's not our age," I add, raising my brow.

"Who cares? He's damn good to look at," Keesh responds, with a giggle.

"I wonder what Fat Daniel and Karli are gonna do tonight?" Steph says, as she files away.

"Did you guys hear the one last night?" I ask.

Amy is already laughing, and blurts out, "Yeah, that was freakin' funny. I wanna take a field trip to UCLA now."

"What happened? I missed it." Keesh questions.

"It was a Hump Night!" The girls are staring at me with anticipation. "They went to UCLA and Fat Daniel pulled down his pants to fake hump a statue of a naked lady. What's even funnier is the statue is...*upside down*." I pause because I'm giggling so much. "Picture it! Hmm...I'm thinking it probably looked like a number...possibly a sixty nine...haha!"

"So is your mom still stalking Ryan or what?" Amy asks.

"Pretty much...this morning she was giving me the low down on all the celebrity gossip...because you know, Ryan says!" I say, mocking my mother. Since Seacrest took over the morning show, my mom has become infatuated with listening. She begins every morning with "Ryan says...." She definitely has a major crush on him. She goes throughout her day talking about Ryan and Ellen, and what they had to say as if they're her real friends. My dad says it's like an affair—an *on-air* affair. I doubt my dad has to worry about Ryan whisking Mom away any time soon.

"Yeah, well the only thing my mom loves more than Seacrest right now is New Kids on the Block," Keesh says, rolling her eyes.

"No kidding, my mom's been going crazy since they came back. I can't believe our moms camped out like little girls just to get their autographs," I add.

"I know, that was nuts. How long did they wait…like over 24 hours, right? Your mom invited my mom and she was devastated that she couldn't go. You would've thought the world was ending with the way she went on. Then your mom came back with a picture with what's his name…" Steph pauses to think.

"Danny!" I fill in the story.

"Yeah, him. She wanted to cry 'cause she didn't get a pic with the one with the blue eyes. It's crazy." Steph snickers, shaking her head. "You know they already have tickets to EVERY concert in the area already?"

Keesh and I nod. Our mothers are lunatics. I don't think I'd ever go insane over a boy band like they are.

"Wanna know what's even crazier? My mom created this virtual city on the guy's website called Dannytown or something. She says all the Danny girls go there and they have official addresses in this make believe town. They're nuts! They even made t-shirts for crying out loud!" I remark.

"Yeah, I think all the women call their fanaticism Obsessive Compulsive New Kids Disorder." Steph tries to sound clinical and then bursts out with the giggles. We all pause, look at each other, and bust up laughing.

Amy finally says, "Okay, your moms are psycho! My mom actually downloaded them on her iPod…but I don't think she has this disorder or whatever." She chuckles. "They have some pretty good beats though. I like dancing to it."

Amy's right, they do have some smooth dancing songs. And if it makes my mom happy, then I guess it's all good. It's just a little weird though. And maybe just a tad bit embarrassing.

But I can't help but add, "You know what though? When I'm my mom's age, I wouldn't mind my man having a slammin' body like Danny's."

The girls all nod in agreement.

Keesh raises her eyebrows and says, "I know right!" She walks over to my radio and turns the volume up a notch. I'm on my feet before the first verse of old school *White Lines* begins. Enough with all the crazy talk about our moms, we need to let off some steam.

It's not long before we're all up dancing, doing booty bumps, calling each other out.

This is *so* fun!

My girls are all together.

No bullshit.

No guys.

No bitchiness

Just us.

Together, like old times.

Who would have thought this would be the last time...for a *long* time?

10

Drill after drill, lap after lap, stretching, sprinting—I thought I'd die before we even get a break. These are try-outs, right? I didn't realize that the goal is to kill the potential athletes before we actually get a chance to play in a game. This is what they call "weeding out" the weak ones.

Kill me now!

Let *me* be a weak one!

Maybe I will get cut. I don't waste any time showing weakness. The thing I feared most actually happens. When I'm dribbling the ball down field, I trip right over it. There isn't even anyone around me and down I go. As I'm trying to control the ball, my foot rolls right over it and I flip into a somersault. Could I look any more retarded?

High school tryouts aren't anything like I've experienced before. Someone please tell me what squat-thrusts or 5,000 sit-ups have to do with kicking a ball into a goal? Nothing, I say—not a damn thing! If I even survive until tomorrow's practice, I may have to reevaluate my decision to take this abuse for an entire season. Maybe I should try-out for something more like the ...the golf team. Don't they get to ride around in a golf cart all day? I doubt Tiger Woods runs bleachers everyday to train.

"So what'd you think of the first day?" Keesha asks, casually. She didn't even break a sweat.

"My quads feel like they're gonna freakin' explode," I hiss. "That's what I think!"

"Chill Meggie, it'll get better tomorrow." She laughs and leans over to push me.

Easy for her to say, she dribbles the ball around the field like a freakin' angel, all graceful, flawless.

"That's *if* I make it to tomorrow. I doubt if I'll even be able to freakin' walk."

"I told you if we were going to take the fall off, we still needed to condition, but you didn't LISTEN," Keesh scolds.

We decided since it was going to be our first year of high school and we had a lot on our plates, we'd skip the fall season of community soccer. We planned on running everyday to stay in shape. Guess who didn't keep up their end of the bargain? Yup...me! Keesha ran every day and I...well...I just thought about running, but I never did.

"Yeah, yeah," I tell her. "Thanks for reminding me."

Keesh and I finish packing up our soccer crap: shin guards, sweaty socks, water bottles, and cleats.

Keesh stands up with ease and holds her hand out to me, "You ready?"

I take her hand for support and she pulls my fat ass off the ground. My legs quiver as they adjust to being upright again. I can actually feel my heartbeat pulsing through my thighs.

"Yeah, we should call Steph and tell her we'll be a while...I think my grandma can walk faster than I can right now," I complain.

"Neither one of your grandmas is alive."

"Exactly," I snicker.

Keesh shakes her head, "You're sick!"

Keesha and I walk to Steph's after tryouts to work on homework. Amy is, of course, out with Alex somewhere. I'm not sure where—she doesn't tell us much. I still talk to Alex, on the phone, but we never bring up Amy—we just talk about school, TV, music, or whatever comes up.

"Let's start with science and get that stupid crossword out of the way," Keesh suggests.

"I already got most of it done before we left class," I tell them. "We only need four across and seven down."

I share what I completed in class and Steph gets one of the answers we still need. We *share* our work. We don't cheat! We have busy lives, other things to do…like watch TV, eat, get online, and now soccer. We can't spend all day working on worthless crossword puzzles or conjugating verbs in Spanish. Not to mention, being in honors translates to piles of homework every night. Not all of it is useless, like the worksheets we get in science though. Ms. Gelson assigns some pretty challenging essays, and in her class, we're expected to reflect on everything we read. I don't think I've ever annotated text in my whole life as much as I have this year. It wouldn't be so bad if I actually liked anything we're required to read.

So, in order to cope with the countless hours of homework, we share…a skill we've been perfecting since we were born. You know, parents are always teaching their kids to share, right? We have just moved beyond sharing Barbies and Poly Pockets—we share…homework.

"Seven down is seafloor spreading," Steph calls out.

"Duh, I can't believe I didn't get that one," I say, disappointed. Even though we share our work, we're still pretty competitive.

"Okay, that's done!" Steph exclaims as she throws her books down and stands up.

"Are you kidding me?" I burst out. "Sit your booty back down, we've got a ton of math."

"Damn, boss. Chill! I got it figured out," Keesh informs us. "Uh-right. Steph, you do one through ten. Meggie, you do eleven through twenty, and I'll do the rest."

Steph puts some music on and we all get started. It sucks not having Amy here—we all have to do more work. How the hell is she doing it on her own? We haven't done our homework by ourselves since sixth grade. Damn, is a boyfriend worth all that homework? Do I even have to ask—this is Alex we're talking about. If he was mine, I'd do all my homework and his. Okay, let's not got carried away again...but I'd at least do mine, all by *myself*.

I only get to number fourteen before my mind starts to wonder. There is a lot to think about. Amy seems to be getting more and more distant, while her boyfriend is becoming more of a friend to me. Alex actually texted me before practice today to wish me luck. How sweet is that! Ben continues to be a flirt and then today, just as planned, I got the chance to speak to Eric during sixth period.

All day long, I had tried to figure out a way to get his attention. Then, the opportunity just fell into my lap.

I guess Ms. Gelson got sick of hearing us talk because today was the day to separate the fab four—more specifically, Ms. Gelson moved *me* across the freakin' room. Why me? *Steph* is the loud one. She may be the nice one, but she's loud as hell— there's not a whisper in that big body of hers. So why was I the one who had to move?

I picked up all my stuff and stomped over to my new seat like a four year-old brat. I was pissed and I didn't try to hide it. That is until I saw who I was going to sit next to. Yup, you guessed it...Eric! Wait...it gets better. We did one of those partner reading things with *Romeo and Juliet* and guess who I was paired up with? Yup, you guessed it again...Eric!

Ms. Gelson really screwed up by moving me next to him. There was no chance I was going to be reading. No chance in hell. It's not like she was going to notice either—most teachers could never imagine such honest honors kids like us *not* doing our work. Ms. Gelson was one of them. She trusted us. What she didn't know wouldn't hurt her. Besides, if she tried to call on me to report our findings, I would be able to BS a decent enough response to appease her.

"So what's up Eric?" I asked casually, or at least trying to sound casual. "I haven't talked to you in so long."

"Yeah, that's 'cause you've been too busy with those senior guys," Eric responded coldly.

I leaned back a bit, in my chair.

"Whoa…I wasn't expecting that," I said, shocked by Eric's comment.

"Sorry," he lightened up. "I wasn't trying to be mean."

"That's okay. It just sucks that it looks like that though. It's mostly just Amy 'cause she's with Alex," I explained.

"Huh…but aren't you with that other guy, his friend…B.J. or D.J. or something?"

He looked down at his book and turned some pages.

I chuckled and blushed, a little.

"Are you serious?" I grinned. "His name is Ben, and no, I'm not *with* him! We're just friends."

"Well that's good 'cause the word is, he's a player," Eric said, with a glare.

That didn't sound like Ben! A player? Ben didn't even have a girlfriend, I had thought.

"You're wrong on that one. Ben's not like that. He's not even with anyone right now," I said, defensively.

"He might not have a girlfriend Meg, but he's got lots of *friends*," Eric said, scrunching his face between his brows.

That was weird. Ben had never mentioned any girls.

But then again, why would he?

"Anyway, enough about Ben. Whatcha been up to?" I asked.

"Nothing really…just school stuff, but I'm trying out for soccer today, you?" Eric seemed more relaxed now and looked at me with interest.

My eyes widened. "Really?" I squealed. "I'm trying out too! Keesh and I both are."

Our classmates looked up at us and Eric leaned in to whisper. "It's supposed to be pretty tough. They only have a few spots on varsity but my game's up so I think I've gotta shot."

Eric smiled as he talked about soccer. You could tell he loves it.

"Ahh Eric, you've got mad skills…you'll totally make varsity." I put my hand on his arm. "Then, you'll have tons of girls calling you."

He gazed at me, put his head down, and said softly, "There's only one girl I want to call me."

He peeked up at me quickly and then lowered his eyes.

My mouth dropped. What was that supposed to mean?

Ms. Gelson interrupted our reunion. She passed out our homework and led a discussion on the day's reading, until the bell finally rang.

Eric and I walked out of class together. We both just looked down, not knowing what to say.

The girls were outside waiting for me. I was one of the last ones out of the classroom since I now sat in the back.

"Hey ladies!" That voice sounded familiar.

Before I knew it, Ben had come up from behind. He put one arm around my shoulder and the other around Steph's. Alex came along and swept up Amy. He gave me a quick smile before walking away. Ben stared Eric down, then nudged us and we all began to head for the doors.

I looked back at Eric and smiled. I felt like crap. It seemed so rude to just leave him hanging there. I shouldn't have let Ben step in and pull me away like that.

However, Ben seemed pretty amused by the whole thing. He knew exactly what he was doing.

I looked back again and Eric shouted, "Meg, remember what I said!"

I looked at him confused.

Which part?

As I walk home from Steph's, after a long night of *sharing* homework, I get a text from Alex.

Hey Soccr Stud! Hows practice??
I smile. Alex is thinking about me.
Good. My legs r stl shakin. I only fell OMA 1 time.
LOL. Whr r u?
Walking home 4rm Stephs...y?
Wanna ride?

Uhhh...ok

Ok...get in.

Huh?

Just as I hit send, Alex pulls up next to me.

"What the heck, stalker?" I joke. "How did you find me so fast?"

"I was on my way home too, and I thought I saw you walking."

I open the door, and flip the handle to move the seat forward. I toss my soccer gear and backpack in the back, and slide in the front passenger seat.

"Well, I'm glad you did. I don't know if these legs of mine could've made it home. I can't even imagine how many miles we ran today. I was ready to quit after the first two. I swear they're trying to kill us."

Alex chuckles, and starts to drive away. "You'll be okay, it's just gonna take a few days to get used to. You should drink lots of water when you get home, that way your muscles won't be so sore tomorrow."

"Alex, I don't have any muscles." I say, seriously.

He glances over at me with a smile. "Everyone has muscles."

"Whatever...I doubt water is going to save me," I reply, massaging my thighs.

"Just do it...for me...please. You'll thank me, I promise," he pleads.

"Okay...thanks coach!" I say, flinging my hand over to smack him on the arm. My hand grazes his and there is instant silence. In that split second, I get the sensation of what it would be like to hold his hand.

Oh my God.

I need to say something.

Come on Meg, say something.

"So what have you been up to? I haven't talked to you in awhile," I say, trying to act normal.

I try not to look at him, but can't help it. I see a slight smile coming from the corner of his perfect mouth.

"I know...you and your friends are inseparable. It's like if I want to talk to you, I've gotta talk to the whole tribe. I still can't believe you were by yourself right now." He chuckles.

"Whatever...it's not like it's really easy to get your attention either," I respond, hoping he'll catch my hint.

"I hear you."

We arrive at my house after I give him the play by play of turns. But I don't get out right away. I stay and talk to Alex for just a bit more.

"So how are classes going?" he asks me.

"ASB is cool. You know that. English is okay too. Ms. Gelson expects a lot, but I'm keeping up. I'm ready to pull my hair out in science. Mrs. C has got to be the most boring teacher I've ever had in my life."

"What about math, don't you have the Mad Hatter?" he asks.

"Yeah, but why do people call him that?"

"You mean, he hasn't spanked the markers yet?" He chuckles.

What? Spank markers?

"Uh...no, why would he spank the markers?" I ask.

"It's this weird thing he does when he makes a mistake at the board. He says 'malfunctioning marker' and puts it in a box labeled 'Mad Markers'," Alex explains.

"That's nuts."

"I know. That's why he got that nickname."

"Okay...that's scary. Now I'm gonna have nightmares about this crazy math teacher throwing dry-erase markers at me or something." I laugh.

"Well, call me if you can't sleep...I'll make you feel better," he says, with a grin.

Hmm...maybe he can't talk to me without leading me on. He sounds like he's flirting, a little. I get the chills and goose bumps pop up all over my arms and legs.

When Alex says things like this, it gets my hopes up. And after the feeling I got when I touched his hand, no matter how slight it was, I don't think I can handle it.

I dig deep to muster up a smile and say, "I've gotta get inside. I bet my mom's counting the seconds before she comes out here to meet you."

"That'd be cool. I'd like to meet her."

I look down at my clasped hands.

"Maybe some other time," I say as I reach to open the door.

I flip the handle on the seat and begin to dig my stuff out of the back.

"Thanks for bringing me home, Alex." I know I'm blushing, but there is nothing I can do to stop it.

"Anytime, Megan. Bye." He smiles, waves, and pulls away from the curb and down the street.

Why is he doing this to me? Why? Why? Why?

I run into my house, throw my stuff in my room, and run to the kitchen.

I need to drink me some water.

11

Alex was right. The water worked and after a few more days, or maybe it was a week, my body wasn't so sore anymore. I actually made the team. Practices aren't as intense as try-outs were so I'm surviving. Barely. But hey...I'm surviving.

I feel like I miss so much while I'm at practice though. Phone calls for one thing. I feel naked on the soccer field without my cell. As soon as it's over, I make a mad dash to finish my homework so I can return all my calls.

"Speak on it," Ben shouts into the phone.

Seriously, this is really the way he answers the phone. Whatever happened to 'hello'? Doesn't that work anymore? I don't know, but the whole I'm too cool *speak on it* bull is just stupid.

"Hey Ben, what's up?" I ask. "I had a missed call from you."

It was weird for Ben to be calling so early. It kind of worries me. He usually doesn't call until late, until I'm getting ready for bed. I wonder what's going on.

"Did you just get home from practice?"

"Yeah, just barely. I hate practicing. Our first game doesn't seem like it'll ever get here. And I still have a stupid paper to write for English," I huff.

"I know, practices suck huh...at least you don't practice year round or have games on Friday nights, like football," he mutters.

I consider that one.

"Whatever! I would love games on Fridays. I wouldn't have to go to school the next day," I complain. "Besides, you know you like the after parties."

"Those aren't so bad, huh," he says, smugly. "That's how I met you."

"Ahhh...how *cute*!" I say, sarcastically.

"Seriously, Megan. It's cool I met you."

What's up with Ben? Is he dying or something?

"Oh...I'm glad we met too."

"That was a cool night." Ben chuckles, quietly. "You know...I thought we were gonna..."

Ben is silent.

Gonna what?

I wait. Still, silence.

"Ben...you there...you thought we were gonna what?" I say, impatiently. He can't just start a sentence like that and not finish!

"Uhhh...I thought we were gonna...gonna hook up." He spits out, softly like he's telling me a secret. "Weird huh?"

"Yeah right," I say. I can't believe he's saying this. "I'm not even your type!" I don't know where that comes from, but I needed to say something.

"Oh...and what's my type?" he asks, defensively.

"I don't know....but not me," my voice screeches. "And if I am your type...why didn't you try anything?"

Ben jumps in loudly, "'Cause Alex would have kicked my ass...that's why!"

"What...what does Alex have to do with anything?" I squeal, with confusion.

"Alex likes you a lot. He thinks you're a good kid and he thinks I'll screw things up with you. He says you're too good for me," Ben explains.

"Really! Damn, Alex doesn't think anyone is good enough for me." *Including him*, I think to myself. "What...am I supposed to die alone and a virgin, or what? Why are you telling me this now?" I rattle on. I can't believe I just said the word "virgin".

And Alex...ugh! I'm so irritated by his hold on me.

Why is Ben even saying anything? What's the point of having this conversation? And why does Alex think that he can tell people to stay away from me?

What the hell is up with that?

"I don't know," Ben pauses. "I guess I just wanted you to know. You've been hanging out with that soccer guy a lot lately. I just wanted you to know you have options."

Options? Options?

Is he serious?

Well, he has a point. I have been hanging out with Eric a lot. He's fun to be around. We have the same classes. We both play soccer. He doesn't care that I suck. And I don't have to deal with any of the older girls acting like I just stole their prized possessions like I do when they see me talking to Alex or Ben.

"Interesting Ben." My tone is serious, my speech slow. "What do you mean by... *options*?"

"Uhh...well you don't have to hang around with that kid so much anymore...we could start hanging out more often."

I can tell he is smiling on the other end of the line. I can hear it in his voice.

"Really...so what...I'm not the nice *kid* anymore? No concerns about tainting my innocence?" I giggle, trying to sound flirty.

"Meg, you're *not* innocent." Ben points out quickly.

"Haha...you got me!"

"So what's the deal with you and sir kick-a-lot anyway?" he questions.

"We're just hanging out...that's all."

I'm not about to give up any info. Why does Ben need to know that I'll probably hang up with him right now and call Eric. He doesn't need to know that I've gone out with Eric a couple of times. Just to the movies, but we've gone out. We're limited because neither one of us is old enough to drive yet.

"Well maybe I'll have to ask you to hang out too." Ben speaks firmly.

There is silence.

"Okay." I'm intrigued yet confused. "So are you asking?"

"Maybe."

"Maybe?"

"How 'bout lunch?"

"Lunch?"

"Yeah, we can leave during 4th and be back before 5th tomorrow. You in?" he asks.

"Sure, why not?" I respond, trying not to sound too excited.

"Hey, I gotta go and you still need to write your paper anyway...so see ya around." Ben hurries off the phone.

"Oh...okay."

"Late." He says, hanging up the phone before I even get the chance to say goodbye or discuss any details.

Wait...wait a minute! What just happened here? I thought my life was going pretty smooth. I mean, my grades are good. Quarter grades are out. I got all A's except for a B in Spanish. Soccer is alright. I survived tryouts and actually made JV. Keesh made varsity, like I expected. Getting moved across the room in English worked out to my advantage. Eric and I have been talking a lot more. I was actually beginning to think I might get my first high school boyfriend. But now Ben has managed to throw another "option" in my love life.

I really thought I liked Eric. Like, really liked him. He is so sweet. He's always saying nice things. He doesn't care that I'm not a size two—that I have some meat on my bones. We haven't kissed or anything—not since last school year. We've come close but I keep holding back. At first I thought it was because of Alex. But that isn't it...he's just a good friend. He's with Amy and I'm over it. Sure, every once in a while he makes me think that maybe someday, we'll be more than just friends. But really, I just enjoy the time I spend talking to him on the phone or texting. It's like I lost Amy, but got Alex in return.

Maybe I'm holding back because of Ben. I've never really thought of Ben like that before...not seriously anyway. Sure, we've flirted, but it's always been...harmless. I've never considered that something might come of it. I just thought we were joking around. But now Ben has asked me out and I can't help but feel little butterflies in my stomach when I think of him. I feel happy, giddy almost.

Why is this happening?

Is this what high school is supposed to be like? I can't stop thinking about Alex. I thought I liked Eric, but now Ben has confused me. He's driving me crazy. They're all driving me crazy! Holy crap! Is it possible to have feelings for two guys? Three guys, maybe??

I have all these emotions going through my mind: confusion, happiness, fear, more confusion, anger...

Wait! Anger...

I pick up the phone and dial.

"Speak on it!"

What's with these guys? That is just so *stupid*!

"Alex, where do you get off telling Ben to stay away from me? Who do you think you are...my mom?" I shout.

"Hi Megan...wanna slow down and tell me what this is all about?" Alex responds, calmly.

And his voice *is* calming—always deep and smooth. I feel a wave of fresh air come over me as I hear his voice. It's almost scary.

"Sorry," I pause. "But I just got off the phone with Ben and he told me some things that bothered me," I say, much softer than before.

"Okay...what'd he say?"

"He told me you said you'd kick his ass if he hooked up with me!" My voice rises again.

I just cut the crap and get straight to the point. I can't wait to hear his side of the story.

"Well, I would," Alex says, so nonchalantly, as if it isn't a big deal.

"I don't get why you'd say that or even think you had the right to."

"Meg, listen to what you just said," he pauses. "You said I'd kick his ass if he hooked up with you. I would if it was just a hook up. If he wanted you, and only you, to be his *girlfriend*, then I'd be okay with it. But I don't think that's what he wants."

Alex is still calm. I'm going nuts. I'm more confused than ever. Maybe it's because I'm a freshman. Maybe this is why freshmen girls should not talk to senior guys. It's hard enough being at the bottom of the high school food chain, but factor in the older, more experienced guys, and I'm going to go insane.

"So are you saying that Ben just wants to hit it and quit it?" I ask, bluntly.

"No you didn't just say that. That sounds so nasty coming from you," Alex laughs.

Why did it sound nasty coming from *me*?

"Why?" I pause. "I think you have this false impression of me. You think I'm this nice innocent little girl or something and I'm really not."

"No, you really are a nice girl. You just think you're bad. Sure, you drink Malibu Rum like its water, go to parties, cheat on your homework, whatever..." Alex chuckles. "But deep down I don't think you're like other girls. I don't think you could hook up with a bunch of dudes, and not care if they didn't talk to you afterward. I don't think that's you."

Well...when you put it that way, I guess I wouldn't be okay with that. I've never even kissed a boy who wasn't a boyfriend or didn't turn in to one. But Alex isn't talking about kissing. He's talking about *more* than that. I've thought about doing more with Eric. I've even thought about what it would be like to do more with Alex. But now, when I think about doing more with anyone, it's just scary. I'm sure if *it* ever happened, I would want something more after. I wouldn't want the guy to just ignore me. No wam bam, thank you ma'ams. But is Ben really capable of being like that? With *me*?

I sit with the phone to my ear, sprawled out across my bed, in silence.

"You there?" he asks.

"Yeah, I'm here," I respond.

"Meg." I love the way he always says my name. "I don't want you to be pissed at me. I honestly didn't think Ben would ever tell you what I said."

"Well, he did," I blurt out.

"I know. I guess I have to beat his ass now anyway, huh."

We both chuckle.

"I don't know," he continues. "You're just different than other girls. You're not fake. You're funny without trying to be. You cuss like a dude but still sound all girlie. You're easy to talk to. I can talk to you forever without all the bullshit, ya know."

"Well, if I'm so freakin' great, then why did you choose Amy?"

It's out before I can take it back. Holy shit! I can't believe I just said that out loud.

He laughs a little. I can almost see the uncomfortable smile on his face. I wish we weren't having this conversation over the phone. I need to see his big brown eyes. They can tell me much more than any of his words.

"Megan, you're too young, and you're…too real," he says.

"Huh?" I mutter. Too young? Seriously?

"I know, I know. You and Amy are the same age, but it's just that Amy and I work…right now. You and I…I just don't deserve you…yet," Alex says, stuttering over his words.

Yet! Yet! Holy crap! These guys are killing me. As if I wasn't confused enough already. Now let's just add one more thing to my madness. And what's wrong with Alex? He always speaks with such confidence and now he's stuttering and tongue-tied. This is all just too crazy.

"Alex, I've gotta go. It's late and I still got a paper to write," I mumble.

"Oh…okay. Hey, I know it's a little weird to talk about stuff like this but…but you're a good friend and I want things to be okay with us. Are we cool?" Alex's voice is soft with concern.

"Yeah, sure…I'm good." I'm really not. "See ya tomorrow."

"Bye Meg."

"Bye."

You know what? I don't have time right now to think about all this crap. I've got a paper to write. Damn, I wish I could do this with all the girls. But papers are off limits for sharing since we got in trouble last year.

I need to talk to Steph, or Keesha, or Amy. Oh shit! I can't talk to Amy. Can you imagine? *Hi Amy, I just got off the phone with your boyfriend and he told me he didn't deserve me.* Seriously. Can you imagine? Ughh!

And Eric...I'm supposed to call him. I take out my cell and text him:

TTYL. Havent finshd my papr n dont wnt 2 stop til I finsh.

I tear open my backpack and yank out my binder. I completed my outline earlier so it shouldn't take too long to finish this stupid paper. I push the power button on my computer and wait—thinking about all I've heard today.

Has anyone ever died of confusion?

There's always a first for everything, right?

12

My right knee shakes frantically with impatience during first and second period. I feel like I'm going to die. Waiting for a chance to talk to Steph or Keesha about my crazy phone calls last night is torturous.

On my way to school, I contemplated my unexpected conversations with Alex and Ben. When I do get to chat with my girls, I know I'm going to leave out some of the details from the convo with Alex—that part about him not deserving me yet, is not necessary to repeat. It makes me feel weird, and I don't want to be mean to Amy by telling anyone what her boyfriend said. In fact, I'm going to try to forget that piece of information. He doesn't want anything from me right now anyway—nothing but my friendship, and that's all I'm going to give. He wants things to be normal so I'm going to try to be as normal as possible.

When I finally get to third period, I'm relieved. We're just doing book work so this gives me the perfect opportunity to tell the girls what happened. I'm going to have to be creative though. We sure as heck can't talk. Ms. O'Brien will freak out if she even hears a whisper. I stare at Keesh and Steph, pursing my lips shut to keep from blurting out my news. I already have paper out, but instead of conjugating verbs, I decide to write them a note.

I grip my pencil, click the top to release some lead, and began to write:

Last night Ben told me I had more options than just Eric. That we could hang out more. We're going out for lunch today. Alex told Ben that he'd kick his ass if we hooked up cuz he thought Ben was just out for a piece of ass. Ughh! HELP! I'm going craaaazzzzyy!!

I pass the paper to Keesha and wait impatiently. My knee is still shaking. As Keesha reads the note, I see her eyes getting big. She smiles and begins to write.

I told you Ben liked you! All that flirting wasn't for nothin'. Stop buggin' and go with it.

I scribble my response and pass it back again.

You're NUTS! What about Eric? And what do you think about what Alex said?

She skims my questions, looks over at me, and rolls her eyes. Then she pauses, looking up at the ceiling before she begins to reply.

Alex is just jealous that you don't want him no more. Don't worry 'bout him. Who says you can't go out with both? Guys do it all the time, why can't we?

OMG! I can't believe she wrote that. These are two nice guys we're talking about here. I can't do that to them. At least, I don't think I can. As for Alex, he's not jealous! He sounded concerned, not *jealous*.

Keesh, you're freaking crazy! I'm not going out with BOTH of them. Actually, I'm not even with either one of them. So we'll just see what happens. I'm just gonna be honest with both of them. Oh, and Alex is <u>NOT</u> jealous!!!!

I write that last part really dark to prove my point.

If you already knew what you were gonna do, what'd you ask me for? And you are going out with both of them. You went out with Eric already and you're going out with Ben today. AND Alex <u>is</u> JEALOUS! Everyone knows he likes you except for you. We all see how he looks at you, even Amy.

I read her ridiculous statements and throw her a dirty look. The space between my eyes crumples with irritation from Keesh's comment. I scrawl out my next reply. She's wrong about Alex, but I guess she's right about going out with Ben and Eric. I guess.

YOU ARE FREAKIN' WRONG! About Alex!

She shrugs her shoulders and passes the note to Steph.

I try to ignore my friends and work on my Spanish. I get a nudge on my arm and look over. Steph holds out the paper to me with a mocking smile.

Meg, I agree with both of you...kinda. Go with the flow with Ben AND Eric. You're not married, you're only 14 so act like it. But Alex does look at you in a DIFFERENT way! Even my sister saw it at the end of the summer when we hung out at my house. He IS jealous but there's nothin' you can do about it now, so leave it alone.

I don't know what to make of everything—especially what they're saying about Alex. But Steph makes the most sense, she always does.

THANKS you guys!

I pass the note back for the last time and wait for the bell to ring. Keesh glances at it, folds it up, and stashes it in her folder. Amy continues to pretend she hasn't seen us passing notes the entire period. It doesn't really matter if she did. It's not like I'm going to show her what we've been writing.

We're all just sitting around in ASB when I get a text from Ben.

hey can u get out erly?

I smile from ear to ear.

Keesh notices my delight. "Is it Ben?"

I nod, and text back.

Sure

meet me otside ur class

when??

now!

I grab my stuff. I can barely find the words to let the girls know where I'm going.

"You go girl," Keesh teases.

"Be careful," Steph advises.

"Have fun," Amy mumbles.

I leave class in a hurry, checking behind me to make sure Mr. Mitchell doesn't see me leave.

I walk outside and scan the quad for Ben. The sun is blinding me, but when I put my hand up to shade my eyes, I see him. He's leaning up against the building across from mine. He looks cute, standing there with his hat flipped backwards, and his arms crossed over his chest.

I move toward him, consciously trying to walk at a normal pace, trying not to seem too eager.

When I reach him, he puts his arms around me in a tight squeeze. My arms wrap around his waist and rest just above his booty. This feels good.

I can feel his breath next to my right ear. His face is nestled into my hair. He holds this embrace for a minute before saying, "You ready?"

I sigh, "Sure, where we going?"

We pull away slowly and look at each other. This is so new to me. That was not just a friendly hug. I definitely felt something more just now, something exciting.

"You pick. It has to be fast food though, we need to be back before lunch is over."

"Okay, how about Wendy's?" I suggest, as we begin walking out to the parking lot.

"Uh…yeah…a frosty sounds good."

"Totally, and we can dip our fries in them." The thought of scooping up the chocolate ice cream with my fries is making me drool just thinking about it. I have the technique down perfectly, it's like art.

"Dip your fries in ice cream? That sounds gross!"

"It's awesome, you've gotta try it!"

We get into his car.

"Okay, whatever you say," he replies.

We have such little time to sit down and eat even though I left class early. We quickly order French fries and Frostys. Ben follows my lead and dips his salty fries in the thick chocolate ice cream. The combination of sweet and salty is just perfectly delicious.

"Not bad," he says, nodding after his first bite, then grabbing another fry to dip again.

In just minutes, we shove our fries in our mouths, and hardly chew. It's nice to go out with Ben, but it would be even better if we weren't in such a hurry. It's kind of hard to make small talk when you're trying to finish your lunch in record time. We start heading back to school before I'm finished chewing my last bite.

As Ben pulls out of the restaurant parking lot and onto the street, he reaches over with his free hand and puts it on top of mine, which is resting on my thigh. I don't move my hand. I don't move at all. I just look down at our hands for a moment, then relax into the seat, with a small grin and an exhale.

We arrive at school and are still in the same position. He hasn't moved his hand and I haven't either. I thought he would when he had to turn, but he drove just fine with one hand. Finally, he removes his clammy hand from mine and we get out of the car.

"That was fun. Thanks, I had a great time." I say, as I walk around the car towards him.

"Yeah, it was..." Ben begins, but is cut off.

"Hey Ben!" some guy shouts. "We've been looking all over for you." He begins to walk over with two girls. Cheerleaders, I think.

"Meg, I gotta go. I'll...I'll call you later okay," he mutters, as he turns his back to me and jogs away.

WTF! He didn't even give me a chance to say goodbye, again! What is that all about? We had such a great time and he ruined it.

Guys! They're stupid!

13

After going out with Ben that day, I've been pretty much doing what the girls suggested. I still talk to Ben. I still talk to Eric. But Ben doesn't make it easy though. He always pops up right after school as Eric and I walk out of English together. He makes it a point to put his arm around me and steer me away from Eric, as if Eric doesn't even exist. I always feel guilty, but I don't know how to make it right. Well, I do know how to make it right. I just can't bring myself to tell Ben to stop. Ben has this intoxicating pull over me. He's such a smooth talker, slick and addicting. One look at his blue eyes and I'm in a trance. And Eric never says anything—he doesn't have to. I can see the disappointment and anger in his eyes every time Ben shows up.

My only uninterrupted time with Eric is during lunch and after soccer practice. Ben always kicks it with his crowd during lunch—Amy is usually with them too. It seems like the only time she joins us for lunch is when Alex is busy or absent. But Ben always stays with his friends and he never asks me to join them, so I don't. We haven't gone out for lunch again since that one day. Ben never did explain why he took off so suddenly.

So at lunch, I just enjoy my time with Eric—and some of his friends that have started hanging out with us. There's Jonathan—cute, soccer player too—who, I think, Keesha is trippin' over. She won't admit it but she gets all tongue-tied around him which is totally out of character for Miss I-Don't-Give-a-Shit-About-What-Anyone-Thinks-I-Tell-It-Like-It-Is. Then there's Josh—he's supposedly this freakin' baseball prodigy who'll make varsity as a freshman—and I think he likes Steph, but she won't show she's interested even if she is.

All of the emotions spinning through my mind are insane. The wheels are constantly turning. Luckily, I have a lot to keep me busy or I'd go mad. This last month in ASB has been jam packed with tasks needing to get done—getting ready for the Homecoming Rally and Dance has been ridiculous. You would think we were planning the opening ceremonies of the Olympics with the way Mr. Mitchell barks orders. He has been running around from committee to committee with a clipboard and a checklist—he's been the rally version of Bridezilla. Seriously!

Steph and Amy's committee has been working hard on the rally. The theme is "Divas"—which means the members of the Homecoming court will impersonate some famous female singers. Jen, Amy's sister, made court with her professional posters and rally tags—she's going to be Mariah Carey. The two cheer monsters, Vanessa and Destiney, also made court, and are going to be Christina Aguilera and Brittany Spears. Is Brittany even a *diva*? Really, come on now! She's more like a freakin' lunatic.

Lydia is getting my vote for queen. She's the most likeable out of all of them—the least clique-ish and the least fake. She talks to everyone on campus, it doesn't matter what grade you're in or what group you belong to. Lydia is going to be Shakira—unlike Steph, she has the perfect body and hair to pull it off. She really does have hips that don't lie!

The last girl to make court is this goth chick, Brittany, who surprised everyone when her name was called. I even heard people say "who?" I don't know much about her but she's going to be Madonna, probably 1980's Madonna with black lace gloves and torn shirts.

I'm surprised we've even had any time to look for dresses before the dance. It's been crazy. We've been staying after school to work on the décor for the rally and dance, and soccer practice hasn't been easy.

So yes…we're all going to the Homecoming Dance. I'm going with Eric. Can you believe it? I'm going to the dance as a freshman. This is kind of a rare thing, for ninth graders to go. It's pretty surprising since we can't drive ourselves, and I'd die if our parents had to take us. But Lydia volunteered to chauffeur all of us peons in her parent's Suburban. So yes…that means that the rest of the girls are going too. Steph is going with Josh and Keesh is going with Jonathan. I already know it's going to be a great night since our dates are close friends. We won't have to worry about anyone feeling left out.

The only one missing from our night will be Amy. Surprise, surprise. She's going with Alex so she'll be with the seniors the entire night. And Ben? I guess he's not going. I put off Eric for as long as possible, trying to hold out for Ben to ask me, but he never did. Every time I mentioned homecoming, he changed the subject. I don't know what the deal is—I know he can dance, so what's his freakin' problem? When I finally told him I was going with Eric, he acted like a jerk. He actually told me I'd be bored and he wouldn't go if he were me. How rude!

It pisses me off that he acted like such an ass about me going. He doesn't want to take me to the dance and he doesn't want Eric to take me either. What…am I supposed to just sit at home like a nerd while all my friends are out at our first high school dance?

It's rally day! How freakin' cool! Today is going to be so awesome! I love ASB. We get to miss our first four classes. We're all excused to help with the rally. What makes it even better is we've all convinced our parents to excuse us from fifth and sixth period too. So when the rally is over, we're going to walk over to the Steel Grill for lunch and then head back to my house to get ready for the football game. Oh my gosh, I hope Lydia wins!

By the time I arrive at the auditorium, it's swarming with students—mostly rally committee members setting up the decorations and blowing up balloons. Keesh and I don't have much to do until tonight's game and the dance tomorrow. Those two events are our committee's responsibility. Instead, we just walk around and wait for show time. Amy and Steph are glued to some spot backstage taking care of last minute details. They look like the real stage hands with headsets and clipboards. I wonder if they even know what they're doing.

As we cruise around backstage, I catch a glimpse of Ben going into the guy's dressing room.

"Ben," I shout.

He looks back at me, half-smiles, and keeps walking. He doesn't stop to say anything or flash me one of his big smiles. In fact, he looks at me like I'm a stranger. What's his problem? What's he even doing here in the first place? He's not in ASB.

Whatever! Keesha and I make our way to our seats in a section taped off for ASB—right in front, of course. It isn't long before the rest of the student body files into the auditorium for the big show. I take some time to soak in my first real rally. The others don't count. They consisted of stupid class competitions that were usually rigged so the seniors could win. We've been told the homecoming and backward's rallies are the best. The skits are supposed to be awesome, so I can't wait to see them.

The auditorium looks incredible with giant pictures of the princesses and the divas hanging from the ceiling. The amount of glitter used to spell out "The C-High Divas" can probably fill the football stadium.

Just as the National Anthem starts, my phone begins to vibrate. Some students think this part of the rally is stupid but I love it. The sound of the Star Spangled Banner, especially sung live like now, brings tears to my eyes. It's such a powerful song. When it's over, I take out my phone to discover I have a text from Steph.

MEG DON'T FREAK! BEN HAS A GF! IM SO SORRY!

Huh? I show Keesh the message, she looks just as surprised and confused as I am. I text back.

WTF r u talkng bout?

Seconds later my phone shakes again with a text from Amy:

Meg, I promise IDK anything or I wldve told u. I promise!

I barely read that one before the phone buzzes again. This time it's from Lydia.

IDK ethr. Just so u no…Bens an A$$HOLE!

What the hell are they talking about?

Keesh smacks me and points to the stage. What is Ben doing up there?

"I'd like to announce our first princess, Vanessa Reyes, escorted today by her boyfriend, Ben Calloway. Vanessa enjoys going to the movies, eating Mexican food, cheerleading, and talking to her boyfriend Ben on the phone for hours every night. Please give a hand for our Princess Vanessa." Everyone cheers as the couple does their catwalk across the stage, ending up front and center.

I'm only two rows back with my mouth hanging open and tears filling my eyes. Ben and Vanessa's smiles radiate into the audience as the students cheer. It's chance that Ben's eyes meet mine. His smile disappears for a split second before he continues playing his part.

Keesh put her hand on mine.

WTF is going on here? My mind replays every moment from the first time I met Ben until just now—in slow motion like a suspense movie. I guess now I know why Ben doesn't call me until late at night. He has to talk to his freakin' girlfriend first! Oh…and at least now I know why he didn't want me to go to the dance. Did he think he could keep this from me? Did he think my friends wouldn't tell me about it? Well…hell…I guess he did a good job of keeping this a secret until now. I'm such a dumb ass! Crap…it was Vanessa in the parking lot that day when he left me hanging. Damn it…I'm an idiot! Vanessa is an idiot!

The rally continues but it's silenced by the thoughts going on in my head. The rest of the princesses are announced, including Jen and Lydia, but I can't bring myself to cheer. They all do their skits but I can't even yank myself out of this trance to pay attention.

High school sucks!

Guys suck!

The rally is over. Keesh stands up. She looks down at me with a frown.

"Come on. Don't even trip! He's not worth it anyway. Everything's gonna be okay," she says as we walk, arms linked, out of the auditorium.

"Don't worry 'bout me...I'm good. Ben can do whatever he wants. He doesn't owe me anything. He's not my boyfriend. We're just friends, remember? It's no big thing," I say, fighting back the tears that are beginning to well up in my eyes. I didn't realize how much I liked him till I saw him on that stage.

Time seems to fade away as we head to the Steel Grill for lunch. It's like one of those out of body experiences you see on a haunted house documentary. I'm going through the motions, but it's like I'm not totally here. If there is such thing as an afterlife, this is what I'd imagine it to be. Things are going on around me, but it's like I'm not really part of it.

We eat lunch first. Then we get ready for the game. I don't even pay attention to Alex playing like I usually do. At halftime, the goth chick is crowned the queen. I'm not in the mood for ASB work, but I do what I have to do and give nothing more. I try to act as normal as possible, but anyone who knows me knows I'm not okay.

Amy and Lydia both spend some time apologizing for not giving me the heads up. Heads up for what? It's not like Ben was my boyfriend. I guess they just figure they should've known something since they're around him so much. They say they were surprised themselves, that they really had no clue Ben was with Vanessa.

Why didn't anyone know about this? Why was it a secret? I mean...Amy hangs out with these guys at lunch...doesn't Ben do anything with Vanessa at school? Oh well...it doesn't matter. He has a girlfriend. He is going with her to homecoming. I'm going with Eric. I just thought Ben was a good friend. I guess he isn't. He hasn't even called me. Can you believe that? He hasn't even called me! You would think he would've at least called, especially

after the way his face went blank when he saw me staring at him at the rally.

Why did he bother taking me to lunch? That hug! Oh my gosh, that hug! It was perfect. Why did he hold my hand? Why? I don't get it.

Whatever...I'm over it. Yeah right!

14

It's Saturday. I wake up to Ne-Yo singing to me—well...he isn't really singing to me, it's my ringtone. Steph is calling me.

"Hey, we're all gonna meet at my house at 7:30. I already called Eric to let him know, so you just need to get here okay," Steph sounds out of breath, but still loud as hell.

"Oh...okay," I say, still groggy. "Is everything okay? You sound like you're breathing heavy."

"Yeah, I just ran a mile. I wanna sweat off as much as I can before I have to squeeze my big bootie into that dress."

We both chuckle.

"How you doing Meg? Do you feel better today?" she asks, concerned.

"Totally. I'm not gonna let Ben ruin my night. Eric's hot and he's a freakin' awesome kisser, so I'm gonna have some fun with him and get my freak on with my girls. So you better be ready. Don't worry about me, okay." I tell her, giving myself a pep talk.

"That's my girl!" Steph squeals. "Hey check with your mom about what time you have to be home...we might go to Denny's or something after the dance."

"Oh...okay. I think she'll be cool with whatever."

"'Kay...see ya at 7:30."

"'Kay, bye."

I roll out of bed and spend the rest of the day with my mother going through the whole beautification process. We go for a mani-pedi at one of those cheap salons—you know the ones where the ladies speak Vietnamese to each other while they clip your toes. Then, we go to the mall where a male hair stylist gives me an updo. Seriously, a dude is doing my hair for homecoming.

When we get to Steph's house, my mom goes in and hangs out with all the parents. They're all there gushing over us and dying to take pictures. We all look great, really. The guys look nice in their suits. I wonder how long they will last at the dance in their jackets and ties. The girls look just as I had pictured—pretty much the same as we did in the dressing room at the mall, but with a lot more make-up and better hair. Keesh, Steph, and I opted for more practical dresses—pretty, but inexpensive. None of us were willing to spend our parent's mortgage or car payments on an expensive dress that would only be worn once. Amy, on the other hand, got her dress from some fancy mall in L.A. She was adamant about making sure no one else would be wearing the same dress as her. I'm sure she looks great. But she and Alex aren't going with us so I'll have to wait and check her out at the dance.

My dress is all black, strapless, and flares out from just below my boobs. The lady in the store called it an empire-waist dress—it's supposed to be a good style for girls my size. The fit is actually flattering once I strap on my heels. They make my legs look a tad longer. I can use all the help I can get. Eric's suit is all black as well. He looks really handsome with his hair all gelled and spiked. He smells good too. I've never noticed he wears cologne.

After several camera flashes and a plethora of poses, we all pile in the Suburban for the dance. I feel like a celebrity being hounded by the paparazzi with all the pictures that are taken. I take comfort in knowing we don't have to work the dance after all. Mr. Mitchell called us this afternoon to let us know all the decorations were finished and we could just come to the dance when it started. I was relieved at the time but maybe I could've used the distraction.

The music is already bumpin' when we get here. We only arrive about forty five minutes late. Lydia said it sucked to be the first ones there so we take our time. We all stop at the check-in table to hand over our tickets. We get the friendly-frisk from security, and take pictures, *again*. The last pic we take is a group picture, just the freshmen till Amy spots us and jumps in the picture with Alex. Whatever!

Eric holds my hand and leads me onto the dance floor. Just as we make our way to the center, along with the rest of our friends, the music changes to a slow song.

"Shall we?" he asks. He smiles at me and puts up his arms.

"Of course," I respond.

I blush, setting my hands on his shoulders, as he pulls me in closer. For the first time since yesterday morning, I feel good. It's nice being in Eric's arms. What's he wearing? He smells so good.

We move slowly, back and forth, getting closer and closer as I hug him tighter. He's much taller than me, even with my heels. He leans over and nuzzles his cheek next to my ear as I bury my face in his chest. I don't know what comes over me, but I look up and gently kiss his neck. It sends flutters down from my head to my toes. He leans back, smiles at me, and continues dancing.

I feel my cheeks get warm as blood rushes through my body. I can feel my pulse getting faster and faster. I take a moment to look around for my friends. I wonder if they noticed the kiss. Instead, I see Ben, staring at me as he dances with Vanessa. Her back is toward me.

How can he look at me that way? Especially when they're so close they may as well be one person. Ughh...my night has gone sour. The whole out of sight, out of mind thing was working until now. Just one glance and the anger, sadness, and embarrassment saturates my thoughts. I was such a fool to think he actually liked me.

The music changes to hip hop and the crowd goes wild. Eric and I separate and begin to dance. I try my hardest to look like I'm having fun. The night started off so nice. I don't want to ruin it for Eric because I'm such an idiot.

For the rest of the night, I force myself to avoid looking in Ben's direction. I do *not* want our eyes to meet again. I haven't even talked to him since the rally, so I'm not about to start now. Not that he would even want to talk to me.

The dance ends and the crowds herd out into the parking lot. We have a big group so by the time we all get to the truck and make it inside Denny's, the place is packed. We walk in and it's standing room only as we wait to be seated. When we finally squeeze into a corner to wait, I take a second to look all around.

Holy shit! I have the worst luck ever.

Ben and Vanessa are standing right behind me. I mean right behind me, like we're almost touching. Eric must notice too because he quickly puts his arm on my shoulder. Everyone else just watches us, like they're waiting for something to happen. Do they seriously think I'm going to flip out or what? Seriously, come on now. Even Alex looks worried. He nods at me. He casts an "it's going to be okay" smile my way.

It sucks that the place is so packed because I can almost feel Ben's breath on my neck. We're like freakin' smashed so close together. What did I do to deserve this torture?

Hang on just one minute! What the hell is that? I look down at my hand that is hanging by my side and see Ben's index finger gently tucked inside my palm.

"Are you freakin' kidding me?" I shout at him as I swing around and hit him in the chest.

"What's your problem?" Vanessa yells, as she gets in my face.

"Why don't you ask your stupid boyfriend?" I shout back.

Everyone is now staring at us.

"Ben, what's she talking about? Do you even know her?" She knows he does.

"Yeah..kinda...she's one of Lydia's little sister's friends. Don't even trip, it's nothing," he mumbles to her softly but I can still hear. *I'm right here, you jerk!* I want to say. Everyone can hear his absurd comment. It's so quiet at this point, you can actually hear the hum of the cash register.

Lydia's little sister's friend. That's what I am to him.

"Dude, you're such a frickin' punk, man!" Eric snarls.

"What the hell did you just say?" Ben pushes Vanessa to the side and gets in his face.

"Ben! Chill!" I hear Alex's voice as he steps between them.

Ben and Eric glare at each other, taking heaving breaths of air with their fists clenched at their sides. Eventually they back off and calm down.

Alex relaxes as well. His focus unexpectedly changes to me. He sweeps my hair out of my face with the tips of his fingers, then cups his hand on my cheek, and smiles.

I look up and gaze into his soothing eyes.

"Hey Lyd, let's go somewhere else!" Alex shouts to Lydia, our eyes still fixed on each other.

I hear her yell back, "Sounds good!"

We break our stare, and set out with our friends to leave Denny's and Ben behind.

Alex is still at my side. Eric is now walking with Amy.

"I saw what he did," Alex says.

"He's an ass," I mutter.

"I guess now wouldn't be a good time to tell you I told you so," Alex laughs.

I smile.

We walk a few steps in silence.

"Alex," I croak, holding back tears. "Thank you."

15

"I'm sorry but I just need to go home," I whisper to Eric, as we pull out of the Denny's parking lot.

"That's okay, I understand," he replies, looking straight ahead. Is he mad at me?

"Hey Lyd, can you drop me off at home before you guys head to the next restaurant? Please," I shout to her.

"No problem," she calls back.

I'm just not in the mood anymore to keep putting on a show. I'm not sure if the rest of the group saw what happened and I'm not ready to hash out the details—which will be the first thing they ask about once we get to wherever it is we're going next.

Lydia pulls up to my house and Eric opens the door to let me out. Keesh and Steph murmur goodbyes and I thank Lydia for driving us. I'm glad that none of my friends pressure me to talk or try to convince me to stay out with them.

"It's too bad the night couldn't have been different," Eric says, softly. "I should knock that guy out the next time I see him."

"Don't waste your time," I say. "Eric, thanks for everything. I had a good time tonight."

I stand on my tip-toes and he leans down to hug me. I hold him tight and give him a quick kiss on the cheek. He hugs me tighter, before letting go with a sigh.

"Bye."

"See ya," he mutters, as he gets back in the truck.

Lydia waits till I get in the house before they pull away.

I'm barely through the front door when my mom appears.

"So how was your first dance?" she asks, with a smile. I can tell she has been waiting for details. This is the kind of thing my mom lives for. She thinks high school dances are like Cinderella's ball. No princes or glass slippers here. Shit, with my luck, I'm surprised I didn't turn into a pumpkin at midnight.

"It was fun...we danced." I shrug.

"I didn't expect you this early, I thought you'd take advantage and stay out late."

"Denny's was packed so we just decided to go home," I remark. "I didn't expect you to be back from the concert this early either. What happened? Danny didn't meet you after the concert for a midnight rendezvous? How was it anyway?"

"They were awesome. What can I say? They still got it, the *Right Stuff*," she gleamed. I thought she was making a joke, but with the way she's acting, I think she's serious.

"Alrighty then." My mom has gone mad, I think to myself. "I'm gonna go take all this crap off...all these pins are driving me nuts." I scratch my head.

"I can help," Mom calls as I walk down the hallway. I'm trying to act normal but she can probably sense that something is wrong. Moms have a knack for that kind of stuff.

"Let me get this dress off first," I yell back, as I turn the corner to my room.

I begin with tossing off my dress and getting into my favorite pair of sweats and a hoodie. It isn't really chilly out but I need the comfort. I walk back to the living room so my mom can begin the process of taking my hair down. It's such a chore to take out all these bobby pins, some coming out easy, some hiding and getting tangled in my hair. Just when I think we're finished, one more reveals itself causing my mom to begin her search again.

As I walk into my room, my phone is buzzing and about to fall off my desk.

I pick it up and hit *View Now*. It's a text from Alex.

R U AWAKE??

I quickly text back.

YUP!

...Buzz...

Can I cll u?

I text him *yes* and wait for my phone to ring.

I pick up the phone as soon as it starts to vibrate, anxious to hear his voice.

"Hi," I say.

"How ya doin'?" he asks.

"I'm good," I respond. "How was dinner, or breakfast, or whatever you call it?"

"Oh, we didn't go after all. It was getting late and I wasn't feelin' it anymore. I wasn't in the mood to sit around and talk."

"So why you calling then?" I ask. "If you're not in the mood to talk."

"Well, I don't mind talking to *you*," he says, softly.

"Well good, 'cause you're the only one I want to talk to right now anyway." I start to tear up, hoping he can't hear the frog in my throat.

"Hey, Meg, don't let Ben get you down okay," he says, in a concerned tone.

"You know, it's stupid. I have this nice guy who actually likes me and wants to spend time with me and I'm getting all worked up over a guy who was just playing with my head." I pause, the wheels turning in my mind. "But then again, what did Ben really do...he wasn't my boyfriend. He never really told me he liked me...just some stupid thing about options. And then lunch...did you know that we went to lunch?" I ask, almost afraid of what he's going to say.

"Yeah, Amy told me. I wish you had told me though."

"It wasn't anything really. It was after we talked that night about you kicking his ass, if we went out. Well, it was great until Vanessa showed up," I scoff. "How stupid am I?"

"So you want me to whoop his ass now or what?" Alex chuckles.

"No, you nerd. Can you believe I didn't even realize why he left in such a hurry until I saw them together at the rally?

"No one knew. I didn't even know. He probably kept it from me on purpose."

"Well I thought I was okay...but then tonight, he was staring at me when I was dancing with Eric...and then him touching my hand at Denny's, what's the deal Alex? What the heck is Ben thinking? Is this some stupid game he plays with stupid freshmen girls, or what?"

Alex doesn't respond right away. Maybe he is waiting to see if I'm really finished.

"Megan, you're not some stupid little freshman, relax. It's Ben who's stupid."

"Thanks. But...but...why is he acting this way?"

"He really liked you. I think he got scared when you starting talking to Eric. He's a jealous kind of guy and I think he just took himself out of the game. Maybe he was scared that you wouldn't pick him over the freshman. He'd feel like an ass if you did that."

I think about that for a minute. "Did he actually say this or are you just guessing?"

"Ben doesn't have to say anything to me," Alex replies. "I know him too well."

"What about the thing at Denny's?" I ask, needing more of his insight.

"That was pretty whack what he did, right in front of Vanessa and Eric. And to you. I don't know what he was thinking." He clears his throat. "Maybe he saw how beautiful you looked tonight and couldn't resist. He could've done worse."

Did Alex just say I looked beautiful? OMG! He is beautiful. How do I respond to that?

"Alex...you think I'm...beaut...beautiful," I stutter.

"Uh...yeah."

"Oh my gosh, you're crazy," I reply.

"Meg, you are...seriously...and the fact that you don't realize it only makes you cuter," he insists.

"Cute...I can handle *cute*," I joke. "Well, whatever that was...Ben's an idiot."

"That he is." Alex agrees. "So, what are you gonna do now...who is it that you really wanna be with, Meg?"

You! I want to say, but I know I can't. I always put my feelings for Alex aside, in a separate place in my heart. They are in there fighting to come out, tearing through my mind and wanting to spill out into words, into actions. But, that can't happen, not now. Not while he is with one of my best friends.

"I don't know," is all I can manage to mutter.

"You know, you don't have to hook up with anyone. You don't have to have a boyfriend," he suggests. Easy for him to say when he has a girlfriend.

"Yeah, I know." I say. "Alex, can I ask you *anything*?"

"Go for it."

"Besides the fact that Amy is gorgeous and has a smokin' hot body, why are you with her? She's definitely not as...*nice*, as you are."

"I have to admit, I'm like every other guy...I was attracted to her body, but she's not as bad as you and your friends make her out to be. When we're alone, she's pretty cool to be around. She's not as secure as you think. She acts normal, fun, just chill...you know." He tries to explain to me, but I don't get it. But maybe I don't want to get it. It's easier to be angry with her without acknowledging that she is a great person.

Amy really used to be a terrific person, but once she started sprouting long, lean legs, and C-cup breasts, she changed. She began shopping brand name labels only and showing off like crazy. We all felt like she looked down on us for not shopping at all the expensive stores or getting professional weaves whenever we wanted. Even if my parents could afford all that, it's just not my style.

"Meg, hello?" he says, loudly.

My mind must have wandered. "No, I don't know...so that's it then, just chill, huh. Do you love her?" I ask, wishing I didn't. Do I really want to know the answer to that question?

"I like her, a lot," Alex states.

"Hmm."

"So, do you feel better now?" Alex asks.

"Yeah...yeah, I do. Is that why you called? To make me feel better," I tease.

"I thought I'd try."

"Well, it worked. I'm good," I say, with a smile.

For a moment, we listen to each other in silence. I feel like I need to say something or like he wants to say something, but we both just...exist, together.

Eventually, Alex breaks the silence. "Well, it's getting late, so I better go. I could probably fall asleep on the phone listening to the rhythm of your breathing. It's kinda relaxing, like those kid songs that put babies to sleep. Umm, what are they called?"

"Lullabies?" I offer.

"Yeah, you can put me to sleep with your lullaby," he says, jokingly.

I smile. "You don't want to do that, you'd wake up with a kink in your neck," I exclaim.

"You're weird, Meg." He chuckles.

"I try."

"You don't have to."

"Ha ha, gee...thanks, Alex." I giggle.

"Okay, I'll talk to you tomorrow."

"What, I thought you wanted me to put you to sleep with the musical melodies of my snoring," I say, kiddingly.

"I said the rhythm of your breathing, I didn't say anything about snoring." He chuckles more.

"Well, you're missing out...I was going to work myself up into full blown concert."

"Maybe next time." He laughs softly. "Good night, Meg."

"Sleep tight, Alex."

"Don't let the bed bugs bite," he adds.

"Okay, Merry Christmas."

"Wait...Merry Christmas? What the?" Alex responds, confused.

"I couldn't think of anything else," I say, laughing quietly, trying not to wake my parents.

"You're nuts!" He laughs.

"I know!" I have tears in my eyes.

"Happy New Year!"

"What?" I ask.

"That's all I could come up with." He laughs more.

I bust up. "Okay…seriously, good night…we could keep going forever."

"Okay," he groans.

"Good Night, Alex," I say, with a smile on my face.

"Sleep tight," he says, laughing again.

I try not to laugh. "Byyyye, Alex!"

"Fine…bye, Meg."

As he hangs up the phone, I can hear him laughing faintly in the background.

I stare at my phone smiling, replaying our conversation in my head.

I roll over and go to sleep with happy thoughts about Alex, hoping those thoughts will invade my dreams. Hopefully he will make an appearance as more than just my good friend.

16

A few weeks have passed since that hideous Homecoming Dance. My friends have been walking on eggshells around me like I'm on a freakin' suicide watch or something. I swear...I'm fine. As if I'm going to let some jackass I've only known for like three or four months get me down. And I didn't even really know Ben...not like I *thought* I did. Alex tried to warn me. Eric tried to warn me. But did I listen? Noooo...of course not! That, my friend, would've been too easy.

Besides the near throw down between Eric and Ben at Denny's, the only other thing people are talking about is the fact that Brittany what's-her-name won Homecoming. It didn't even phase me the night of the football game. All I was still thinking about was the great unveiling at the rally. Now that I've had time to think about it, I can't believe that chick really won. Seriously...how did they even know it was her with that black curtain of hair covering half her face. She's like a dang Cyclops— you can only see *one* of her eyes. She reminds me of Violet from *The Incredibles*—only in skinny jeans and black nail polish. Apparently, this is all the rage at my school and I didn't even know it.

Cyclops and cartoon characters. This is what I'm thinking about. I'm such a loser. Tonight I'm just chillin' at home, trying to relax after my first soccer game. Both JV and varsity won today, which made for a wild ride back home in the bus. Since it was an away game, we didn't have much of a cheering section, but I was actually relieved. I would've been way too nervous to play well with a bunch of people from school watching.

Buzz...buzz!

That's my phone. I can feel it somewhere. I search all over my bed. I didn't even hear it start ringing since the volume on my radio is turned up. I flip up my comforter one last time and my phone flies off the bed. I pick it up and flip it open. It's a text.

Congrats on the win. We won 2! Chk ur email...2 long 2 wrte in txt.

Hmmm...what could Eric have to write in an email? Why doesn't he just call me if it's too long to write?

I was just online, checking MySpace, so it doesn't take long to bring up my email.

Meg,

Hey sweetheart! I know you're probably wondering why I chose to email you instead of just calling, but I figured I wouldn't get all nervous if I wrote it. Since we both had luck with our games today, I thought I would try my luck with you too!

So I've just been kicking back waiting to see what would happen between us or to see if you would end up with that punk Ben. But now it looks like Ben showed you what an ass he is, so I don't think I have to worry about him anymore.

Anyway, I know we had a thing last year, but this time it seems different. I like you a lot. I love being around you. Everyone does...that smile of yours makes everyone smile too, even when they don't want to. You've gotta know how I feel about you...it's not like I haven't shown you. But I need to know how you feel. Do you think of me the same way? Damn, I hope so...

Can you just tell me...will you be with me? and ONLY me? Don't play games with me, okay or try to spare my feelings. Be honest...if I'm not the one you want, tell me now, please!!

Thinking of you....

Eric

OMG! Why does he have to be so sweet? My head is so full of crap from Ben still that it's not letting me enjoy this wonderful email from a *nice* guy. Remind me to go to the junior highs and tell the girls to stay away from the seniors next year. By this time, shouldn't I have had like five boyfriends already? Isn't that the way high school is supposed to work?

I put my face in my hands and take a few deep breaths. I can feel a pinch of pain in between my eyes. Great, I'm getting a freakin' sinus headache. Now is not the time.

Relax!

Eric is a great guy. He's nice. He's funny...he buys me Ben & Jerry's Chocolate Fudge Brownie ice cream even though I don't need it. He likes to hang out with me and my friends during lunch. Well, his friends are trying to get at mine, but still.

Shit! If we don't end up together, it'll really screw up our lunch time routine, won't it? Will Eric, Jonathan, and Josh still hang out with us if I say no to him? Everyone will *hate* me if I screw this up. Crap!

I click on *Reply*.

Hi Eric,

You have got to be the sweetest guy in the world...or at least at Carver...don't want you to get a big head or anything. So you like me, huh? And you love to be around me? You like my smile too? Damn, I pretty lucky to have someone like you, aren't I?

Well I'm not gonna shoot you and put you out of your misery today..no such luck! I think you're stuck with me 'cause I really like you too and I can't imagine who else I would like to spend my lunchtime eating Baked Chips and drinking Naked Juice with! Plus, who else is going to help me improve my soccer game? Well, let's not base our relationship on my ability to play soccer. We'd be doomed.

No...seriously. Of course, I want you! And ONLY you!

"You complete me!" (get it...Jerry Maguire... "you had me at hello"...haha...I'm so funny)

So boyfriend...is that what I should call you now?? I gotta go. I need to take a shower and get rid of all the grass and dirt from my crevasses.

I'll talk you tomorrow!

Dreaming of you...

Meg

I read my email twice before I hit send. What else can I possibly say? We have a good thing going. I can't ruin it...not for me...not for Eric...not for our close group of friends. It *has* to be this way. I'm not *completely* lying. I can see the potential to feel like he's the only one I want. There is definitely that potential. If I can just get that LOSER out of my mind...things will work out here. Really! Really?

My inbox makes a sound. One new message.

You had me at hello! Haha! Just kidding! You had me when you pouted like a little kid 'cause Ms. Gelson moved you to your new seat. Remind me to thank her!

Good night!

I smile. This might work...

17

Thanksgiving break flew by leaving very little time for me to hook up with my friends, or Eric. My mom is a nut when it comes to shopping so we were out at four o'clock in the morning on Black Friday—along with many other psycho people seeking a $20 DVD player or "buy one get one for a penny" sales. It's crazy, I know...but it's actually kind of fun.

Steph was totally busy with her family during break—relatives came in from Arizona and Texas for the week—with her mom giving both her and Lydia a long list of things to do. Mostly, they had to entertain all of their younger cousins while the adults did their thing. Steph didn't complain though.

Amy stopped by my house to visit Thanksgiving Day. I wasn't too surprised. Her mother doesn't cook—they buy their holiday dinners. So Amy usually makes her rounds to visit all of us. I know she loves her, more fortunate, situation when it came to shopping for clothes or getting the perfect salon highlights in her hair, but when it comes to holidays, I know she's jealous. She envies the family gatherings and nurturing mothers the rest of us have. So she popped in and I let her soak in the smell of a freshly baking turkey and a real sense of family, not just money!

Keesh was actually pretty scarce throughout our break. Normally, she would've been the one to get us all together, at least once, but she was preoccupied. It wasn't Jonathan either. I asked Eric about it and he said that Jonathan had hardly talked to her. When I finally got a hold of her, she said she was hanging out with some of the girls on the soccer team. The varsity girls. Well *excuse me*.

Eric spent some time at my house Thanksgiving Day. He actually ate dinner with us. It seemed a little soon to have him over for a holiday, but my mom insisted. She likes what she sees in Eric so far. He's polite on the phone. He walks me home after practice and my mom said she noticed a "skip in my step" when I announced I was with Eric, again.

At dinner, he made himself even more likeable. He pulled my chair out for me and made small talk with my family. That really impressed my dad. And when we were finished, he helped clear the dishes. Eric is what all mothers hope for. He's definitely growing on me!

After such a peaceful Thanksgiving Day and a tiring weekend of shopping, I actually can't wait to get back to the routine of school.

"How was practice Meggie?" Keesh asks as we start taking off our gear.

"Alright...I guess," I say, yanking my sweaty socks from my feet. "At least, I can walk now when we're finished."

I laugh and throw my dirty sock at her.

"Gross...that's sick!" She throws it back. We both giggle.

"Hey Keesha...we gonna go to your house or what?" this tall Amazon-like girl asks.

"Yeah...hold on...I'm almost done," Keesha tells her.

"So, you must be Megan." She waves at me.

"That's me...wassup!" I smile.

"Oh...Meg this is Nicole...Nicole this is Meg." Keesha points at the both of us.

"So are you coming Meg?" Nicole smiles at me.

"Uh...where to?"

"We're going to my house...wanna come or are you waiting for Eric?" Keesha asks, blankly. Something in her voice tells me that she'd rather me wait for Eric. That's not like Keesh, at all.

"Why not...Eric went home early today...he wasn't feeling well," I explain.

"Let's go then, I'll drive," Nicole says.

Well, who the hell else is going to drive? As if she doesn't know Keesh and I can't. We stuff our crap in our bags and stand up. I slide my flip-flops on and follow Keesh and Nicole out to the parking lot.

This is weird. Nicole seems to know who I am but Keesh has never mentioned any of the girls on her team. They're acting like close friends. I guess it makes sense though. I mean...if you spend every day after school together for three hours, you are bound to become friends. I already knew most of the girls on my team because we're all pretty much the same age. But the varsity team is mostly seniors, except for Keesh.

"So where is everyone?" I ask Keesh. It's very quiet in her house which means we're alone.

"Mom and Dad went to the gym."

Nicole opens up the slider that leads to the backyard. She makes herself at home, as if she's been here many times before. Keesh follows her.

"You coming Meg?" Nicole asks, slyly, raising her brow.

I walk outside and shut the door.

I stand there as Nicole takes out a little purse. Why in the hell is she gonna fix her make-up after practice? My face is probably still red from running up and down the soccer field. It usually stays like that till I go to sleep. No amount of make-up would help.

Wait...wait a minute...

"What the hell is that?" I shout.

I kind of have a feeling but I'm not really sure. I'm not too experienced with this sort of thing. Actually, I'm not at all experienced—but the knot in my stomach tells me this is not good.

"It's a pipe," the words roll off Nicole's tongue. "What...you've never seen one?"

"No actually, I haven't," I state. "What are you gonna do with it?"

I guess I don't need to ask because she takes out a small black film canister and puts a pinch of something—that looked like a mixture of bay leaves and oregano—into the pipe. Before you know it, she pulls out a lighter, puts the pipe to her lips, and lights the small little bowl at the end on fire.

WTF!! WTF!! Seriously...WTF!!

"Is she smoking..." I turn to Keesh.

"Chill Meg, it's just a little weed...it's no big thing...really." Keesh shrugs her shoulders and takes the pipe from Nicole. She lights it up like an old pro.

WTF!

I turn and walk right inside. Keesh is too into her new friend to follow.

I take out my cell and start to dial Eric. I shut my phone. What the heck can he do? I flip it open again and dial.

"Speak on it," Alex says. That is so stupid.

"Hey Alex, are you busy right now?" I ask.

"I'm at Amy's...why what's up?"

"I need a favor, but you can't tell Amy, okay?" I wait.

"Sure, you sound upset...what's wrong...it better not be Ben." His voice starts to flair.

"No, no, nothing about Ben. I'll explain when you get here. I'm at Keesha's. Can you pick me up from here? I'll be outside waiting, 'kay?"

"I'm on my way." Alex hangs up.

I open my phone again and text Alex directions to Keesha's house.

I get my bags and walk out the front door. I look back. Keesh doesn't even check to see if I'm still here. Or to ask me to stay. Or to see if I'm okay.

I'm so pissed. I can't even bring myself to wait outside. I fling my bags over my shoulder and start walking toward my house. I text Alex again to let him know where to find me. My heart is beating like a time bomb.

Not even ten minutes have passed before I hear the Golf pull up along side of me. I walk toward the curb, open the door, toss my stuff in, and jump inside.

I look up into Alex's big brown eyes and start to cry.

"What the heck Meg...what's wrong? Are you hurt? Did someone hurt you?" Alex says, with fear, clutching my arms in his hands. He turns me toward him, looking me over like he's inspecting me for signs of violence.

"No...no...I'm okay...just a big nerd I guess." I'm still crying, but laughing too, in between sobs.

"Meg...you're not making sense...tell me what's going on." He releases his grip.

"Well...I just saw one of my best friends doing drugs and I freaked out," I say, my teeth beginning to chatter. I'm so scared, I start to shiver. "I've never seen anything like that before...I'm such a wimp." I shake my head and frantically wipe the tears from my eyes.

"Okay, so what was she doing?" he asks.

"I guess Keesh has this new friend from soccer. Her name's Nicole. We went to Keesh's house after practice and Nicole took out a pipe and started to smoke weed. Then, Keesh did it too."

Is this really happening? It doesn't even seem real as I tell Alex the story.

"Huh...I don't know what to tell you." Alex searches for the right words. "When you get into high school, things are just different...your friends are different. Sometimes people do things you wouldn't expect them to. You just need to make a choice about what you're gonna do." He smiles. "But it looks like you already made that choice."

"Well, I wasn't gonna stay there and smoke out with them...I don't know why I got so freaked...I just felt like me being there was wrong. I know I don't always do the right things but smoking dope out of some funky pipe thingy just doesn't seem right," I explain.

"So...now we know...you're a lush...just not a pothead!" He slaps my thigh, jokingly, and laughs. Even though he's kidding, the touch of his hand on my thigh sends a million tingles through my body.

"Oh gee...thanks...you make me sound like I'm one drink away from AA meetings." I smack him back, laughing. My body's still tingling from the slight contact I had with him.

"So, you better now?" He puts his hand on top of my mine. The tingling intensifies.

"Yeah...I'm sorry I called you...I just panicked and dialed your number." I pull my hand out from underneath his and wipe my eyes again, trying to calm the jitters he's making me feel.

"Nah...don't even trip...it's all good. I'm glad you called. I'm glad you let me be here for you."

"Oh crap...I'm sorry I asked you to lie to Amy. Do you think I should tell her?" I ask, seriously.

"Hey...don't worry about it. I just told her I had to leave. She didn't know it was you on the phone. Should you tell her, I don't know. It depends on what you want her to do or what you think she'll do," Alex explains.

"Honestly, I don't know what I want. I don't even know what to say to Keesh. Maybe I need to talk to Steph and Amy so we can figure it out together. I think this one is beyond me," I say, defeated.

My eyes start to tear again.

"Keesha is lucky to have a friend like you. It'll all work itself out. Are you ready to go?" he asks.

"Yeah...can you take me home?"

"Sure," Alex says, as he starts his car and takes off down the street.

We get to my house quickly. I gather my things and open the car door.

"Thanks Alex...thanks for everything. You're always saving me." I laugh.

"I don't mind the job." He winks. "Call me if you need me."

"Thanks." I grin, and shut the door.

I walk into my house and straight to my room to throw down my stuff.

I take out my cell phone and begin texting:

Do me a favor. Next time you wanna hit the pipe, don't invite me. I'm NOT interested.

18

I wake up feeling conflicted—my thoughts are torn with sadness, distrust, and *fear*. What the heck happened yesterday? It was truly upsetting. I can't believe this is bothering me so much. Teens do drugs all the time—I even know some of them. Shoot...a few kids were even trying stuff in elementary school. But this is different—I had never even seen any kind of drugs up close like that, or anyone doing them right in front of me. I've never even seen anyone doing drugs at the parties we go to—those who are interested in that stuff find some place away from everyone else to do their business. My circle of friends has never been into that, so naturally, I've never seen anything myself.

Now I feel like everything has changed. I went to Keesh's yesterday thinking we were going to just kick back and work on some homework. The next thing I know she's *packing a bowl*—I think that's what I've heard people call it—and inhaling marijuana from a pipe. All she needs is a syringe, a spoon, and a rock and she can be a real junkie—I've never experienced that sort of thing in real life either, only in the movies. But still, this is crazy. And no wonder so few kids get caught with drugs at school because their stuff is so easy to hide. That pipe was so small it could fit in the palm of my hand, and I have really small hands.

I take a shower, dress, and go down to the kitchen. My mom is there already, engrossed in her daily routine: coffee, English muffin, and the love of her life, Ryan Seacrest, on the radio.

She notices me shuffle in and says, "Good morning! You must've had a restful night. I didn't hear your cell beeping every five minutes like usual."

Why is it that she notices my cell phone not buzzing, but she never notices that I come home *drunk* from football games...well, sometimes anyway? How do parents miss these things? How do Keesh's parents not know she is doing drugs? How did I not know one of my best friends is doing drugs?

"I was tired so I turned it off," I explain.

"What's up honey? Did you get in a fight with Eric? Sometimes you just have to be patient, boys don't always know the right things to say or do, *Ryan's* the only guy that'll admit that."

Oh great. She's talking about Seacrest again.

"No Mom, Eric is perfect. I was just tired," I lie.

"Oh, are you sick? Don't you feel well?" She is now concerned.

"No Mom, I said I'm fine. Just tired from so much soccer practice," I tell her.

I grab my whole wheat English muffin and a bottle of water and walk out of the kitchen.

"See ya later," I call out.

"Okay, bye." I hear faintly.

I debate on whether or not to tell Amy and Steph. I don't think either one of them knows. Keesh is still giving Amy the cold shoulder because of Alex. I don't know why 'cause I'm totally okay with him and Amy now. Really, I am. And I'm not even lying to make myself feel better. I'm really okay with it. Did I mention I'm okay with my best friend dating the guy I loved all summer long? Really, I'm okay!

And Steph...she would've been more freaked out then I am so I'm sure she would've said something. She would've definitely told me that our best friend had traded ice cream and Cheetohs for the *herb*!

I've decided not to run and tell Amy and Steph what happened. I'm going to see how things go today...see what Keesh says and how she acts. I guess I'll take it from there.

Things seem pretty normal during class. Same ol', same ol'. Lots of review since finals are coming up right after winter break. We just got back from Thanksgiving and we're already getting ready for Christmas vacation.

This year is flying by.

At lunch, Keesh seems to be her normal self. I keep staring at her eyes looking for clues that she's high. I don't know what I'm looking for but I've always heard you can tell by looking at someone's eyes.

Eric takes out his hacky sack and starts to kick the little mesh bag around. He is pretty good, landing it on his knee, the top of his foot, and bouncing it up again. I can barely volley a huge soccer ball, I don't know how he manages that tiny thing. But he looks good doing it.

"Hey Eric...you're pretty good at that," Alex says, as he and Amy walk over.

Alex joins Eric, Jonathan, and Josh, while Amy sits down with us.

What are they doing here? They never sit with us during lunch...

"Wassup Ames...whatcha doing on this side of the tracks?" Keesh snarls.

"Alex saw Eric kicking that thing and wanted to come over to play," she explains.

Oh...this was Alex's idea. I have a feeling it has more to do with Miss Pothead over here than with playing kick ball with the guys. If I know Alex, like I think I do, he stopped by to check on me.

"So...all it took was a hacky sack to get you to hang out with us again, huh?" I joke with her, trying to squeeze out a laugh, although I think I'm the only one who thinks it's funny.

"Yeah Ames, it's cool to have you around," Steph adds.

"Whatever," Keesh mutters and joins the guys. "Hey Eric...I bet I can keep it up longer than you can," she shouts.

"I hope *not*!" I yell.

Everyone stops and stares at me, including Alex.

"Hey...I was just *joking*!" I yell again, embarrassed.

"It's too bad you're just kidding, Meg." Eric winks at me.

For a split second, I'm beginning to forget about my drug addict friend. Wait...maybe we should start calling her Mary Jane.

We watch them play, in complete silence, and after a while Alex comes over.

"Break time," Alex sits down with us on the grass. "How's everything goin' ladies?" he asks, looking directly at me. I'm right, he's checking on me.

"Good," I respond. Then mumble, "So far."

"Good to hear," he says with a nod. "Amy, we should get back and get our stuff before the bell rings."

"Oh, okay," she says. "Bye guys, see ya in a bit."

Keesh runs over. "*Bye* Amy, so nice to talk to you," she jabs.

Why is she being so freakin' rude?

Fifth period come and go, as does sixth period.

Eric and I walk out of English together, as usual.

"Meg!" Ben smiles and nods at Eric. "Looks like you settled for second best, huh?"

My face immediately scorches with anger.

"No...Ben...honey...if that was the case, I'd still be waiting around for your dumb ass."

I stand on my tip-toes, peck Eric on the neck—that's as far as I can reach—grab his hand and walk in the opposite direction.

I knew a confrontation with Ben was inevitable. I'm actually surprised it didn't happen sooner and it wasn't much worse.

"Sorry babe," I say, as I look up in his eyes.

"Don't apologize." Eric smiles. "Thanks for calling him a dumb ass...but I could've come up with something worse."

He leans down and kisses me on the side of my forehead as we walk.

Moments like this make me forget about all the other drama in my teenage life.

19

I love winter break! It comes at just the right moment every year. Just when my brain is fried and I don't think I can endure any more, two weeks of mindless relaxation and snuggling up to my wonderful boyfriend is the answer to my prayers.

I don't know why I even came to school today, the day before break—we haven't done anything all morning, just party after party. We're not having Christmas celebrations though, these are all *cultural experiences*. Cultural smultural...I know why I came to school today...Eric. It's really happened...I love that guy!

By the time lunch comes around, I can't eat another thing. I think I polished off an entire container of those brownie bites with powdered sugar on them. They're so addictive. The delightfully moist sweet little squares were just calling my name and I couldn't say no. Now, I'm just lying down on the grass with the back of my head resting on Eric's thigh. I'm even contemplating undoing one of my buttons, my stomach is that full. Shit...I can even feel it in my neck. I think I have brownies stuck in my esophagus. Seriously.

"Hey Keesha...you gonna come or what?" Nicole asks, looking only at Keesh.

"Yeah." Keesh stands up. "I'll see ya guys later."

She walks off with Nicole and doesn't even wait for a response.

Oh no, she didn't.

But she did...she just left with that sasquatch stoner.

"Who is that? Where is she going?" Steph questions.

"I don't know." I'm in shock.

I'm not sure what to say to Steph.

The bell rings not too much later and we're off to P.E.

Keesh doesn't show up to gym.

She's a no show for English.

I dodge Steph's questions during P.E., which is pretty difficult because she's very persistent, but I can't hold back anymore.

I have to make a choice.

My *choice* is to tell my friends that one of us has taken up a new hobby.

"You guys...I've got to talk to you about something," my voice cracks.

"Hey hon...what's wrong?" Eric puts his arm around me.

"It's about Keesha," I say.

"Where is she anyway?" Amy asks.

My friends are staring at me. Everyone else in class is talking too, even though we're supposed to be eating quietly while we watch *Romeo and Juliet*. But Ms. Gelson doesn't seem to mind since it's just a party day.

"She took off with some tall chick during lunch," Steph says, confused. "But I don't know who it was or where she went."

"I think I do." I put my head down.

Eric squeezes my shoulder. "Megan. Tell us what's going on."

"She's on drugs." Amy states.

"What?" Steph screeches.

"You *know*?" I ask.

"Wait...Keesh is on *drugs* and you both knew, but didn't tell me," she lowers her voice to a whisper.

"Sorry Steph...I found out and I didn't want to believe it and I didn't know what to do. She's been acting normal so I thought maybe she just did it once, but now I think I'm wrong," I cry, trying to catch my breath.

I try to keep my voice down and my face hidden because I don't want to draw any more attention to our group than I already have.

"Come on, that's not the type of friends we are...we don't just let each other do stupid shit and not say anything. We talk about everything. It was real stupid not to tell us...we're better than that." Steph shakes her head with disappointment.

"What's she doing?" Eric asks.

"She's smoking weed with her soccer team," Amy informs them.

How does she know this?

"Amy, how did you know?" I ask, wiping the tears from my eyes.

Damn...I'm such a baby.

"Jen told me," she explains. "She heard some rumors and let me know. She said I could do whatever I wanted with the information but she doesn't want to get involved. I know how both of you get...look at you Meg, you're crying and you didn't even do anything wrong. So I thought I'd try to take care of it myself and then I'd tell you guys."

"So did you come up with anything?" I ask her, because I have zilch.

"I told Keesh I knew and I was going to tell her parents if she didn't stop," Amy went on. "She's been smoking with them since Thanksgiving. That's why she didn't get us all together like usual. That Nicole chick is something else. When I confronted Keesh, Nicole cussed me out and Keesha didn't even say anything."

"So that's why she's been a total bitch to you then," Steph exclaims.

"That and I told her parents," Amy mutters.

"You did *what*?" I'm in shock again. "What did they say?"

Amy continues, "Keesh's mom was really upset, and her dad got pissed. I seriously thought Keesha's mom was gonna kick Nicole's ass. Both her parents thanked me and told me they'd handle it from here, so I just haven't said anything else."

"Holy crap!" I say, loudly. "What do we do now? She skipped both periods with that stupid witch."

"Hey, you ditch all the time Meg." Steph reminds me.

"Yeah...to go to the Steel Grill, not to get...high," I shoot back.

"Chill you guys," Eric insists, trying to quiet us down.

"I'm gonna ask Ms. Gelson if I can go to the bathroom and I'm gonna call her mom. If we don't do something now, she's gonna be with those chicks all during break and who knows what's gonna happen."

Amy stands up.

"Are you sure you want to?" I ask. "I could call."

"She already hates me," Amy says. "She doesn't have to get pissed at you guys too. I won't even tell her you guys know about it."

She walks over to Ms. Gelson, then leaves the room.

"This is some shit," Eric says.

"Tell me about it." Steph and I mutter at the same time.

Gosh...how could I ever be so rude to Amy? Look at what she's doing for Keesha. Look at what she's doing for all of us. This is the old Amy I know. This is the sensitive, caring Amy that was fun to be around before we had to grow up. I feel guilty now for giving her such a hard time and for thinking bad thoughts behind her back.

20

Word travels fast because when I get home early from soccer practice, both my parents are waiting for me with...a DRUG TEST! Yes...I said a drug test. See, my friends and I have been in the same classes for years. Fortunately, or unfortunately, whatever you want to call it, our parents have gotten to know each other *really* well. That's how it works with honors students. Back to School Nights, Open Houses, Report Card Pick-up—it doesn't matter which event, our parents always run into each other because we have the same teachers. We usually use this to our advantage because our parents trust each other and never bother to check up on us...until now.

"Sit down Megan Ann Miller!"

Oh Shit! My dad used my whole name!

And he's home early.

This is not a good sign.

"Okay. What's going on Mom? Dad?" I ask, worriedly.

"Keesha's mother phoned and told us what's going on with her," my mother explains.

I can tell she is uncomfortable with saying out loud what is really going on with Keesha. I feel the same way. This is not a conversation I want to be having with my parents.

"Did you know about this Meg?" My dad asks.

"No," I start to lie, but then I quickly change my mind. "Well yes, I did but I just didn't know what to say or do."

My eyes are drowning in tears already. I can feel them swelling up with each second.

"Are you doing the same thing as Keesha, Megan?" my mom asks with her head down.

I think she is crying too. I can hear soft sniffles coming from her direction.

"Nooo!" I cry out. "You think I'm that stupid. I went to her house to do homework and she and her new friend starting smoking weed. I freaked out and left. I was there for less than a minute once I saw what they were doing. I wouldn't do something like that."

Once I started talking, I couldn't stop. I can't even believe they even asked. Sure, I'm no saint but I don't do drugs.

"Well then..." Dad says, firmly, "you won't mind if we ask you to take this drug test then, right?"

He pushes a box across the counter. I pick it up and look at it. It *is* a drug test—just pee and you get the results. Seriously...like the pregnancy tests they show on commercials. Is this what this world has come to—over the counter drug tests?

"Whatever...sure," I laugh, sucking back my tears.

I don't have anything to worry about.

I read the directions and I'm off to the bathroom. Within minutes, the results are in...ALL CLEAR! I'm drug free! I'm so relieved even though I already knew what the results would be.

My parents look relieved as well. Did they really think I was a druggie?

"Well, I'm happy with the results. I can't say I'm surprised. But I'm still disappointed," my mom expresses.

"Why Mom? I don't do drugs!" I raise my voice.

"Meg, your friend was in trouble and you didn't say anything. Amy is the one who came forward. You guys all give her a hard time for being this spoiled brat, but she was the one who had the courage to help Keesha. She was the one who called her mom...you did nothing." She ran her trembling hands through her hair, then wiped a few tears that were falling down her cheek.

It hurts me to see my mom like this. I really disappointed her. It's not a good feeling to have.

o o o
125
So I'm a Double Threat

"There's no excuse...but I was scared. This doesn't just happen every day Mom. It's not like a math test, I wasn't prepared. I didn't know what to do." I cry even more. I need them to let me off the hook for this one. I can't deal with their disappointment.

"It's been a long day. Why don't you just get some rest? I'd like you to plan on being home till after Christmas, okay. It wouldn't hurt all of you to spend time with your families. We'll see what comes next, after the holidays," Dad explains.

"Do you know what's happening with Keesha?" I ask, concerned and curious.

"Uh...Kendra said they have a good family doctor so they're gonna take Keesha to see him. I guess they're gonna go from there based on his recommendations. I have a feeling she will be at home all of break. Maybe you should just give her family some space for now...give them a chance to figure this out. I'm sure Kendra will keep us updated," Mom responds, calmly.

"Alright, I'm gonna go call the others." I stand up to leave.

"Megan...if something like this happens again, please talk to us," Mom pleads.

"Sure thing," I say.

As I walk to my room, I hear the door bell ring. I open it to find Amy, Alex, Eric, and Steph. What are they all doing here?

"Whoa...what are you guys doing here?" I ask.

"Kinda just happened we all had the same idea...I guess," Steph speaks up first.

"Weird, huh?" Eric says.

"You think your parents would be cool with us coming in?" Amy asks, shivering.

I didn't even notice when the weather turned cold. It's like we skipped fall—going from the summer heat to the winter cold without anything in between.

"Come on in, everyone," my mom shouts from behind me. "I figured you would all find each other at some point. Who's this though?" She looks at Alex.

She has definitely heard of him, but she has never met Alex personally.

"Mrs. Miller, this is my boyfriend, Alex." Amy introduces him.

"Oh. Hi Alex, I've heard a lot about you." She shakes his hand.

Did she really have to say that?

"Hey kids...I can fix a fire for you outside if you want to talk out there," my dad offers.

Since when did my parents get to be so cool? This is not the norm.

I look at my friends and then we follow my dad outside. We grab some chairs, unfold them, and place them around the fire. It's chilly out, but the burning embers and the crackling of the wood makes it warm and cozy.

"Hello, Mr. Miller, my name is Alex." He holds his hand out to my father.

"Hey Alex, nice to *finally* meet you," my dad says, with a little too much emphasis on *finally*. Not Dad too! Is this a conspiracy? I hope Eric didn't notice that. Maybe my parents know more about me than I thought.

"I can get us some drinks before we get settled," I tell them. "I'll get some sodas."

I run in the house and return to find everyone already talking about Keesha. My parents are inside watching TV so we have some privacy. I'm anxious to see what everyone knows about what happened to her.

"So what's the story?" I ask, passing out cans of soda, and then sitting down next to Eric.

He puts his hand on my leg just above my knee and I feel much better for the first time today.

"So, Keesh's parents actually had to go looking for her because she wasn't answering her cell and she was nowhere to be found," Steph speaks up loudly, catching everyone's attention.

Amy continues, "When Kendra called my mom to tell her what was going on, my mom asked Jen if she knew Nicole. Jen was just as worried as the rest of us so she told Kendra about this empty house next to school where a lot of kids go to do drugs and stuff."

"So that's where they found her?" I interrupt.

"Yeah," Amy continues. "Kendra actually called the school and the police...there were a lot of other kids from school there and a lot of the varsity soccer girls too. A crap load of people are getting suspended, and kicked off the team."

"You didn't hear anything at practice?" Eric asks. "All the guys were talking about it on my team."

"No...I left early, remember? Plus, nobody said anything," I tell them. "I didn't notice anything either. This is big. I can't believe so many people are involved."

"Don't be so naïve, Meg." Alex looks at me intently. "This school is full of drugs. Take a look around every once and awhile...really. Just because none of us are doing them, doesn't mean they're not there. Actually, there's a stat that almost fifty percent of twelfth graders in the country have actually smoked marijuana before."

"I'm not naïve Alex," I say, defensively. "I guess I just never paid any attention because it's not like I'm interested in doing drugs. Damn...that statistic means that out of all of us here, at least two of us will smoke weed by the time we're in twelfth grade."

There is silence.

"I have already," Alex says, slowly looking at each one of us in the eye.

"Me too," Eric admits.

"Are you guys kidding?" Steph screeches. "You guys aren't *bad* kids. *We're* not bad kids. We're good students. We're not supposed to do stuff like that." I can tell this revelation is upsetting to her.

Steph hangs her head low. She is sad and disappointed.

"I tried it last year," Eric explains. "I was at a friend's house and someone took out their stash. Everyone tried it, so I did it too. I didn't like the way it made me feel though...just lazy, dead, and hungry. So I never did it again and don't plan on it."

I look at Eric...trying not to think of him differently. I'm glad that he's being honest. I trust that he's serious about not doing it again.

"Yeah...it was pretty much the same with me." Alex begins to tell his story. "But Ben and I did it a lot our sophomore year. We got comfortable at school, playing football, and hanging out with seniors. We tried it after a game and I liked being relaxed, but we just did it too much. All I wanted to do was kick back and eat, everything was funny, and my grades sucked. I had to take summer school for the last two summers to make up for it. We both got lucky...we got sick of it and we just stopped. But a lot of my old friends still do it...well, they're not really friends anymore. People who smoke weed or do other drugs don't hang out with sober people...it's a buzz kill."

"Wow Alex, I had no idea," I'm really surprised by this news. "So what do we do about Keesh?"

"Nothing." Alex blurts.

"What do you mean nothing?" Amy says.

"We can't just do *nothing*," Steph urges.

"I think Alex means that Amy already did all we can do," Eric explains. "Amy told her parents...now it's up to them and Keesha—actually, just Keesh. She has to make the choice. We just have to wait and see what happens."

"That's gonna be hard," I tell them. "I'm like the most impatient person in the world. It's killing me not to call her right now or just go to her house. This sucks!"

"Be patient, Megan," Alex smiles. "Everything will work itself out...I *promise*."

Eric grabs my hand and squeezes it, looking from me to Alex, and back to me again.

"Alex, that's not something you can just promise," Amy says, coldly.

"You're right." He pats her on the leg, "I was just trying to be optimistic and I am. I really think everything will be okay."

"I hope so." I look at him, meeting his stare. "I hope so."
Eric pulls me closer to him and kisses my cheek.

21

Christmas Day is just like usual. Since I'm the only child, my parents don't bother to wake me. We open up gifts when I get up, which is usually around nine o'clock—not too early, not too late. When I was younger, I would wake my parents around four in the morning because I was so anxious to see what came from Santa. Now, I know better. I mostly get clothes from Aeropostale or Kohl's, nothing fancy or too expensive. Every once in awhile, I might get a new CD, movie tickets, or some lip gloss in my stocking, as a bonus. Don't get me wrong...I love Christmas, but it's mostly for the little kids. They're the ones that get all the cool gifts. I miss the days of getting Barbies or little craft kits with markers, crayons, and chalk.

This year I'm surprised. Guess what I got? Santa—aka Mom and Dad—got me an iPod! A real iPod! Not a fake mp3 player like the one I lost in the bushes with Keesh's tampons...this is a real freakin' iPod! And a good one too! I jump up and down and yell like crazy before I even sit down to really look at it. I just saw the box and freaked. When I finally settle down, I realize my parents bought me a sixteen gig iPod Touch! Yes...the one with a touch screen. The memory is huge—I can fit like a million songs and a ton of movies on it. Actually just a few movies, but thousands of songs. They also got me a $100 iTunes card.

I squeeze both my parents till they beg me to stop.

"We wanted to get you something extra special, Meg," my mom gushes. "We wanted to let you know that we're proud of you for making the right choices."

My face drops—they gave me this expensive gift because I'm not a pothead like my friend. Guilt starts to set in. OMG! They think I'm still their sweet little girl...that I can do no wrong. I look down at my new iPod and look at them. I smile wildly. I can live with the guilt.

I hug my parents again, "Thanks guys!"

It's tradition to go to Amy's for New Year's Eve. Her parents always have a huge party. I don't think they have much fun, but I know they like to show their guests a good time. They cater the best food—appetizers, dessert, and all—and have a huge bar full of liquor and beer. You name it, they have it!

It's usually just the four of us girls who go to the party, but this year it's a little different. Okay...a lot different. Keesha is still on lockdown. Her parents don't let her out of their sight. Another change is the boyfriend factor. Amy has Alex and I have Eric. Josh and Jonathan crash the party too, but they're like one of the girls. They aren't hooking up with Keesh and Steph anymore—Keesh for obvious reasons. As for Steph and Josh...they both just started looking at other people.

Apparently, high school couples have a limited life expectancy when it comes to relationships. The fact that Alex and Amy, and Eric and I, are still together is actually rare. Boys and girls our age seem to be hookin' up with different people every other week. Steph's mom said "you guys all change boyfriends and girlfriends like you change underwear." It's funny and gross, but kind of true.

I like it better being with just Eric, and not a ton of other guys. I can't imagine going out with a guy who has already kissed or put his hands all over a hundred other girls. Gross...all my class mates are probably infected with all these diseases from playing tonsil hockey and sticky fingers. Seriously, that's probably the least of what they're doing—I know tons of kids who are doing a whole lot more than just feeling each other up, above and under the clothes. I'm pretty lucky I don't have to worry about where Eric's *parts* have been.

At the party, we just hang out upstairs in the loft—it's this huge area with a giant entertainment center and big cozy couches. We all kick back, eat, and watch movies. In the past, we would sneak up drinks without the adults knowing, but this year—because of the Keesh thing—we decide to steer clear of the extra-curricular activities. The adults probably wouldn't notice this year either, because they haven't checked on us, not even once.

It's just a half hour away from the new year when Steph has to leave. She always leaves early so she can be home to do the count down with her family. Her parents are weird that way, but I think she enjoys it just as much.

"Thanks Amy," Steph says. "I had a great time...like always. I'm gonna wait out front. My mom should be here any minute."

"We'll go with you, Steph," Josh says, as he and Jonathan pull themselves out of the sofa.

"Where you goin'?" Alex asks.

"My cousin's house for another party," Jonathan responds. "It's probably just getting started. My brother's gonna pick us up. Thanks for inviting us Amy."

"Oooo....," Steph smiles. "Looks like it's gonna be couples only!" She raises her brows up and down quickly.

I look at Eric, then at Amy and Alex. My stomach does a back flip. I'm not sure I want to be here alone with my boyfriend and Amy and Alex.

Steph starts toward the stairs. "Don't do anything I wouldn't do!" she yells.

"Well, that doesn't leave me much," I joke.

"You got that right," Josh smacks Steph on the ass, "This girl is tight with her shit."

She socks him in the stomach, "And you wonder why."

We all laugh hysterically.

"Let's bounce." Jonathan scoots them both down the stairs, still chuckling.

"Bye guys!" Steph yells.

"Bye!" We all yell back in unison.

I can hear Steph and Josh still play fighting all the way down the stairs. Steph doesn't care about a graceful exit. Those two are so cute together. It's too bad it didn't work out.

When we can no longer hear Steph, it's eerily quiet for a minute. The silence is uncomfortable. We're all alone. It's just the four of us. It's never been just Eric and I, and Amy and Alex. It feels weird. What is even more weird...or sick...is that I can *hear* them kissing.

I look over and see Amy already sitting on Alex's lap. He has one hand on her thigh that is draped across him, and the other is at the top of her back. I can't see their faces—thank god—just Amy's hair shielding them like a screen. But I can definitely hear the smacking of their lips.

Kill me now...seriously...kill me now!

Eric pulls me closer. Damn...I hope he can't feel my heart racing. It's ready to explode out of my chest right now. I'm just slightly uncomfortable. We're sitting closely side by side. He has his arm around me and he's running his palm up and down my arm. I have my hand on his leg that is crossed over his other knee. I love stroking his lower leg. His hair is a little curly and coarse, and its texture feels so cool against my fingers. I can sit here all day just dragging my fingertips back and forth over his leg hair. There is something about this sensation that I can't describe. It's mostly just fun to do, but maybe a tad bit sexy too.

Eric kisses the top of my head and I look up at him. He leans in for a kiss and I try to forget that Amy and Alex are just a few feet away doing the same thing. Shouldn't they come up for air? Are they part fish or something? Do they have gills we don't know about?

I kiss Eric anyway—a long open-mouthed kiss with *Alex* right next to me. I focus on the softness of Eric's lips. I usually love kissing Eric. It makes me feel good, too good sometimes—like raging teenage hormone good. But hold on a sec...kissing Eric isn't like that romance smut my mom reads. It isn't anything like the pages of a Harlequin Romance novel—not at all like, "I loved the sweetness of his breath as his lips parted mine and the warmth of his tongue as it thrust into my mouth forcing moisture to flood between my legs." That crap my mom reads is borderline porn.

Beside, does that really happen?

Definitely not with high school boys.

Boys my age don't have *sweet* breath. Okay, so I've only really, really, kissed one boy, but have been near enough to know that their breath is *not* sweet. It's more like a combination of a Monster drink and Hot Cheetohs. Where are these guys with sweet breath? And what about the thrusting tongue? That sounds so *seductive*. Teenage boys are *not* seductive...more like messy and clumsy. The *moisture between the legs* thing is the only thing I can relate to. But that has nothing to do with Eric seducing me...it's just hormones! Hormones...just good ol' hormones making me want to jump into his lap and straddle him like you see in the movies.

I have to hold back...Amy and Alex, remember? Although, it doesn't seem to bother either one of them that we're here.

Or maybe it does? Because just as I'm thinking this, Amy and Alex get up and go to her room. OMG! Are they gonna do *it*? Have they done it *already*? She's a pretty bold bitch to take her boyfriend into her room alone with her parents just downstairs. I can't believe Alex is not more respectful. I'm a little disappointed.

Oh well! What the heck? I jump up and onto Eric's lap, facing him with my legs bent on either side of his thighs...just like a movie.

"Whoa," Eric says, his eyes wild with excitement. "What are you doin'?"

He puts his hands low on my hips and squeezes.

"Shhh!" I kiss him.

I kiss the shit outta him.

And I kiss him some more, with my hands under his shirt, running up and down his bare back and his on mine. Our tongues dance together perfectly. I suck playfully on his lower lip and go back to his kiss. He traces my lips with his tongue and then lowers his head to kiss my neck first gently, then with more force. Oooo...maybe this *can* be like the books. This is as close as we have ever been. Normally, we just kiss, but not this much and *not* in this way.

OMG! I can feel *it*! Yes...*it*! His *thing*! I've felt it before but *not* like this. Normally, it just brushes up against my stomach—he's tall and I'm short, remember—when we are standing up. But now I can feel it well, rock hard like nothing before, right between my legs since I'm riding him like a race horse. Damn...it feels good. He's has these thin soccer shorts on—yes in the winter—and *it* is going straight through my jeans. I thrust my hips into *him*, out of curiosity.

Holy shit! Is this the way it's going to feel? OMG!

I quickly fly off Eric like Harry Potter in a Quidditch match, and just stand there a few feet away staring at him, out of breath. I can feel the heat radiating from down there all the way up to my eyeballs. This is insane.

My bra is undone. When did that happen?

"Wha...what's wrong?" Eric says, his lips puffy, with a tent pitched in his lap. "Did I do something wrong?"

I fix my bra. "No...no...not at all! That's why I had to stop."

"Oh...okay," he says, disappointed. He takes a deep breath and says, "We can just watch TV...sit down."

He pats a spot next to him on the sofa.

"Looks like we missed the countdown," I say, as I sit down and cuddle close to him.

He kisses the top of my head, "Happy New Year, sweetie."

"Happy New Year, babe," I say back.

We sit in silence for a few minutes.

I want to say something.

I just don't know what.

"Well...that was fun," I blurt.

I'm so stupid.

"Yeah...it was!" Eric can't hide his excitement even if he tried.

"Hmmm..." I don't know what else to say.

"So, is this to be continued?" he asks. "Will there be a sequel?"

"Uhhh...I think that can be arranged," I tell him. I really want there to be a sequel. I already want that feeling again. What scares me is the curiosity brewing in my mind about what it'd be like to go further than we did just now.

"So why'd you stop?" Eric asks. I can feel him looking at me.

I look up at him and then look back down, quickly.

"Uhh...I was scared...it was feeling a little too good." I explain.

"And that's a bad thing?"

"It would be if we didn't just stop there."

"You're not interested in doing more?" He pushes.

Eric is very serious.

"Uhh...I'm definitely interested...but also definitely not sure that I'm ready for that yet." He is probably going to dump me. Isn't that what boys do when you say you're not ready?

"That's okay...it's all good," he assures me.

"You sure?"

"I've only waited for 15 years...a little while longer won't kill me," he says.

"Can you imagine...death by blue balls." I laugh.

We're both laughing when Amy and Alex come out. His shirt is all wrinkled and she has the worst case of bed head I've ever seen.

Looks like they were *ready*!

22

"Amy," I mutter. "Can I ask you a question?"

"Sure Meg." She looks at me. "Wassup?"

"Am I sleeping in the spot where you and Alex just did the *nasty*?"

She hits me in the head with a pillow. The guys left and I'm sleeping over. Amy has a queen size bed big enough for both of us to sleep in.

"What was that for?" I hit her back.

"Why would you think we had sex?" she asks, angrily.

"Well you came out with your hair all crazy and Alex's shirt looked like he just pulled it out of his pocket, it was so wrinkled up," I tell her.

"Oh...and you weren't doing anything with Eric?" She sits up, leaning on her elbow, and raises her eyebrow at me. "You're face was all red like you just finished a soccer game and Eric had a *wet* spot on his shorts!"

"Eww...you're sick." I hit her with my pillow.

"Why am I sick?" she laughs. "I'm not the one who got Eric all wet." She giggles more.

"Okay...okay...enough." I cringe.

"So...you guys doin' it or what?" she asks, matter-of-factly.

"No way...you?"

"Nope."

"Oh," is all I can think of to say.

"But I think I want to," she lowers her voice.

"I was thinking the same thing after tonight, but I don't know," I say. "You better get condoms or something...you don't want to end up like that girl on that TV show."

"Oh, I know," she shudders. "Jen told me about this place...family planning. They give out condoms and stuff...or you can get the pill or a birth control shot."

"Are you serious?" I'm curious and eager to know more.

"Yeah," she continues. "They don't tell your parents. You just walk out with a brown paper bag of goodies...no questions asked."

"If it's that easy," I wonder, "then why are there so many girls at school getting pregnant all the time?"

"Because they're freakin' stupid!" she scoffs.

I'm silent.

"Will you come with me?" Amy asks softly. "I just want to be prepared...you know...just in case."

"Where's it at?" I ask.

"Down the street from school...we could walk," she explains.

"Okay," I say, surprising myself. "We can go on Monday. We can skip a few classes and go...just in case."

"Thanks Meg." She smiles.

"You don't have to thank me," I tell her. "Just one more memory we can add to our high school scrapbook. Should we take pictures?" I comment, sarcastically. "What a memory to share with our grandkids."

We laugh and then turn with our backs to each other to go to sleep.

Just walk in and walk out, huh!

No *parents* involved.

Just getting prepared.

Just *in case*.

A brown paper bag of goodies...

Better than a belly full of *baby*.

Ugh!

I squirm at the thought!

23

Like usual, I'm on my way to school...*thinking*. Seriously...I really need to find someone to walk with, so this internal dialogue that forever invades my mind can be silenced.

Today, Amy and I are supposed to ditch a couple of classes and go get *lunch*. That's going to be our code name for it since apparently, where we're going, birth control comes in a brown paper bag. So *lunch* it is!

Just one problem—I'm starting to feel like I'm not ready to *need* lunch just yet. I've been thinking about New Year's Eve non-stop. My night with Eric was amazing. I think about it every minute I'm awake and then wake up with a smile because I've been dreaming about it all night. Seriously...I can't believe how good he made me feel! But at the same time, I'm also feeling a little scared and a little grossed out by the whole thing.

Seriously...I could feel his thing...his *thingy*! Just the fact that I can't say exactly what I felt—I mean the real word for it—is probably some kind of sign. And did he really have a wet spot on his shorts like Amy said? How embarrassing! Did Alex see that too? Ugh! I know it wasn't pee—I think I would be sickened less if it was. How gross...seriously!

OMG! Eric really did have a wet spot on his shorts. Eww! I can't believe I'm totally trippin' over the thought of Eric doing his *business*. If that's the case, then I probably shouldn't be there when he *really* seals the deal—if you know what I mean.

But what can I do? What am I gonna say to Amy? I can't just ditch her in her time of need. I seriously don't think she'd go alone, to get *lunch*. And I really don't think her mother is ready to be a grandma—I don't think that prissy lady ever will be. So maybe I'll just go with her...to make sure *she* gets lunch. We'd better safe than sorry, I guess.

Seriously...this thought just crossed my mind—Amy is going to get lunch so she can have sex with ALEX. OMG! I don't think I had that image in my mind before now. Ugh! Now I'm really going to be sick.

I don't know which makes me feel worse—the thought of Eric and I having sex or Amy and Alex having sex.

Holy crap!

I think I'm gonna be sick, for real.

"What's wrong Meg?" Steph shakes me.

Her brash voice startles me. I'm already standing outside my science class and I have no idea how I got here.

"Oh my gosh," I answer, dazed. "I was just day dreaming, I guess."

"Wassup?" Keesha cries. She smiles at us both waiting for a response. I just stand there.

"Heeeey!" Steph screams and hugs her. "I was beginning to think we were never gonna see you again."

It's true. We haven't talked to Keesha since the last day of school before break, when she left with Nicole at lunch. And now, here she is, acting like nothing happened.

"Hey," I mutter. I don't know why I'm so angry, but for some reason, my blood is boiling like a magma chamber about to erupt.

Keesha hugs her and they rock back and forth. "Tell me about it, Steph," she squeals. "It's seems like forever. I missed you guys so much."

"Hey Keesh," Amy says, plainly. "So did ya kick the ganja or what?"

"Amy!" Steph yells.

Keesh is speechless for the first time in her life, as I am.

"What?" Amy puts her hands up. "What did I say? We're all wondering the same thing. Why not just get it all out now, so we can just move on."

"Well?" Steph says, turning to look at Keesh. Steph's eyes are practically popping out of her skull, in anticipation.

I'm still in shock, standing there staring at Keesh with my mouth open.

Keesh has tears in her eyes. "I gotta go."

We all watch her walk away. She doesn't look back.

"Damn Amy," Steph exclaims. "Do you have to be like that?"

"Don't blame me Steph," Amy warns. "If she can't handle talking about it, how is she ever gonna stop. We can't just baby her. She owes us an explanation. Don't you think she should at least tell us she's stopped...'cause if she hasn't, I don't want to be around her."

"As if you're ever around anyway," Steph shoots back. She pauses, and then says, "You know what...I'm sorry. I shouldn't have said that."

"Seriously," I say, calmly. "Let's just chill. This whole thing with Keesh sucks. We don't need to be fighting and shit right now. Just chill!"

Steph and Amy back down, and just scowl at each other for a sec.

"So we still getting lunch today?" Amy asks me. "We can leave after ASB. That will give us enough time to get there and back before your practice."

"Uhh," I stall. "Yeah, what the hell...let's get *lunch*!"

"You guys are ditching again," Steph cries. "This is our first day back. Talk about addiction."

I think about that for a minute. We really need to be careful. Mrs. Caldwell was starting to give me an attitude about my absences, before break.

"Well, it least I won't get lung cancer or kill my brain cells," Amy teases.

I laugh and add, "Yeah, and we won't gain ten pounds from getting the munchies."

"Haha, you guys are so funny," Steph mocks. She seems irritated at first, but eventually lets out a small laugh.

"Hey babe," Eric hugs me from behind.

I didn't even hear him come up. I turn around and give him a quick peck. He leans in for more but I just look away. Every time I kiss him now, it's like he wants a repeat of the other night. He can't stop talking about it either. I know, I think about it too, but I don't feel like talking about it every second. It's like Eric has become obsessed with creating moments for us to make out with hopes of another lap dance. Now, at this very moment, when he tries to kiss me again, I'm thinking, 'chill out dude, you're not gonna get in my pants at school.' Because, I know that's what he's thinking about right now. I just know it!

"Geez," I push him away. "Relax...frick!"

"I was just trying to give you a good morning kiss," he mutters.

"I gave you one, you don't have to shove your tongue down my throat to say good morning," I argue.

He looks confused, and hurt.

Why am I being so mean to him?

The bell rings. Amy waves bye and Steph goes into class without me.

"I've gotta go. I'll see you later."

I wrap my arms around his waist and squeeze, trying to say 'I'm sorry I'm acting like such a nutcase right now.' I wonder if he can understand my gesture.

He hugs me back and kisses the top of my head. How can I be so freaked out by a guy who can be so sweet like that? Seriously...he just kissed the top of my head. How freakin' cute is that.

Wait! He just made me forget that all he's been talking about lately is me straddling him the other night and what it would be like to do that...naked! Yes, he actually used the word...NAKED! Seriously...this sweet guy can be a freakin' horn dog! No wonder I'm so wigged out.

I let Eric go and walk quickly into class, not even giving him a chance to say goodbye.

I don't see Keesha again until math, where she remains quiet again. She barely even glances in our direction. She walks over to the ASB room alongside us without saying a word. I'm not going to be the one to say anything so I just leave her alone.

ASB is uneventful. Mr. Mitchell is in a meeting with the chairs of all the committees so we're on our own. The four of us just sit on top of our desks, waiting for someone to speak up. Steph is biting her nails, Amy is looking at the tips of her hair for split ends, I'm just fidgety, and Keesh just stares at the floor.

It seems like forever, but it's only been about three minutes before Keesha says, "Okay, you wanna know what's going on...well here it is."

Our heads shoot up, and we just look up at her, wide eyed and anxious.

"Hmm...let's see. I was smoking dope with my friends and my parents come in with the cops and caught me. My friends got kicked off the soccer team. The only reason I get to stay on the team is because I've never been in trouble before. I had to agree to go to this drug, alcohol, and tobacco program so I'll only get a bunch of Saturday schools instead of getting suspended. And my parents put me into some freakin' drug counseling program 'cause they think I'm some frickin' pothead or something. And this is all because you guys couldn't keep your mouths shut!" she says with force and anger, raising her voice with each point she is trying to make. By the time she is finished, she is out of breath and standing in front of us with her hands on her hips.

"Excuse me," I yell back. There is an immediate silence from the rest of the class. "Are you freaking kidding me? You're lucky you have friends like us or maybe someday your parents would have found you with a needle in your damn arm. That Nicole chick is not your friend. Is that the kind of friend you want? If it is, then what the hell are you still doing here with us? It would be a lot easier without you. At least my parents wouldn't be making me take a fucking drug test every week, you ungrateful…" I turn my back on her. I can't even finish my sentence but I think the whole class knows where I'm going.

I have to sit down because at some point while I was yelling I stood up. I can't believe she has the nerve to tell us it's our fault.

The girls just sit there stupefied. It's not like me to tell people off like that, especially one of my girls.

"Can we just chill and not be so loud?" Steph suggests, in a whisper. I laugh inside at this coming from her. I didn't even know she knew how to whisper.

"I'm sorry Keesh, but you're not the only one who has to deal with all this crap. You brought me to your house where you were doing *drugs*. Some people think that smoking weed is no big deal, but it's still a drug. I got into that dumb ass's car and she had drugs in it. If we got pulled over, I could've been arrested. You could've too. Do you get that? Did you think that I was gonna be like 'cool, let me have some'. It sucks that you put me in that situation…so it's not just about *you*," I begin to choke up a bit.

Amy puts her arm around me and says to Keesha, "We're not trying to gang up on you here. You said what you needed to and we should get the same chance."

"Go ahead," Keesha mumbles.

"I just want to say that I called your mom 'cause I love you like a sister. You're one of my best friends and I care about you guys a lot. I was worried about you. I would do it again if I had to. I wouldn't change a thing. I could tell you I'm sorry, but I'm not."

Steph looks to Amy for a signal that she's finished. "So are you done, Keesh? Are you gonna keep doing this shit with your other friends?" Steph asks.

Keesh is quiet. We all stare at her waiting for a response.

"I'm sorry I said those things before," Keesh begins. "It's over. I'm not doing it anymore. It's not worth the grief my parents are giving me and it's not worth losing you guys over. Plus, I've gained like five pounds and I run as slow as Meggie now, so I need to get my ass back in shape." She glances at me, smiles, and begins to laugh.

"Whatever works!" I laugh too.

Steph tackles Keesh and hugs her. Keesh hugs me, then Amy too.

We're such girls!

Now that things are okay with Keesha, how are Amy and I going to explain that we're going to *lunch*? We don't have to worry about Steph, she never wants to leave with us. But Keesh, she's a different story.

"So we leaving for lunch still?" I ask Amy in front of everyone.

"Sure," she says. "You wanna go now or after this lunch is over?"

"Let's go now." I can avoid Eric for, at least, a little while if we skip lunchtime.

"Where you guys going?" Keesh asks.

"We're gonna hit the Steel Grill, wanna come?" I say, looking back and forth at her and Amy. Amy looks like she's going to choke on her gum when she hears me invite Keesh.

"You know I would, but I think it would be better if I don't draw any attention to myself right now," she explains.

"Just be good for awhile, then we'll get back to dumping our bags in the bushes," I joke.

"See ya later," Amy links her arm in mine and we leave.

I look back at them and yell, "Tell Eric I went to lunch, I'll text him later."

So this is it! We're off to get our brown paper bag...our lunch!

24

We're all going to the Backwards Dance—this one is simple to figure out since it's in the school cafeteria. We don't have to worry about anyone taking us, we can all walk there together. The Backwards festivities are pretty much the same as Homecoming, but a lot more casual.

Since everything is backwards, the girls have to ask the guys to the dance. I, of course, asked Eric. Amy asked Alex. Keesha asked Jonathan, and Steph asked Josh—they aren't all back together or anything, they just figured it would be easier to go with our group of friends rather than bringing some new people into the mix. Keesh and Steph save the experimentation with their hook-ups for when the real couples aren't around. It's cool this way. We all got along really well—it would be annoying to deal with any *outsiders*.

Nothing much has changed since Amy and I went to get our lunch. My brown paper bag is still intact in my closet, in a box. I haven't felt the need to take it out. I can't believe how easy it was to get the stuff in the first place. If I didn't care about people knowing I got condoms, I'd make flyers and spread them all over campus so that everyone would know there's a free clinic for teens—so all my ridiculous classmates can stop getting pregnant. Buuuuttt, I don't want anyone to know—I don't even want *Eric* to know or he'll be trying to jump my bones every chance he gets.

Eric can be such a sweet guy...seriously. He does all these things like hold my hand, carry my soccer bag, walk me home from practice, he calls me babe and sweetie...stuff like that, you know. He gives me quick pecks on the cheek or kisses the top of my head, but when we start kissing...I mean, really kissing, he gets all crazy on me again. We haven't had another night like New Years because I get all tense and we stop.

I'm kind of bummed...I started out the school year thinking about *Thunder from Down Under* and having some hot guy's naked body all over me. But now, I go running when my cute boyfriend starts to put his hand on my ass. I'm good with the kissing and even a little bit of rubbing, like that night...but that's not enough. I don't think Eric will want to stop there—I know he wants more. So that's where I'm at...I don't want to eat *lunch* yet...I'm just cool with the appetizers! Why can't guys be okay with appetizers? Why do they always want to jump on the juicy steak first? Did I just compare myself to a cow? Good one, Meg.

As for Amy, she hasn't opened her lunch yet either. I don't know much more than that because she gets all irritated whenever we start talking about it. It's like she wants to know everything about Eric and I, but doesn't want to even mention Alex—which is actually okay with me, because I really don't want to know the steamy details about her and *Alex* either.

It's a good thing. That our lunch hasn't been opened yet. We all survived our first semester of high school without getting pregnant, diseased, beat up, or caught ditching. We've been through some crap with Keesh, but it is all good now. When grades came out after finals, it's no surprise that we all manage to get at least at 3.6 GPA—that stat would've been higher if Keesh hadn't missed so many assignments because she was off getting high.

Like Homecoming, Backwards events include a rally, a football game called Powder Puff—the girls play football and the guys don a cheerleading uniform—where the king is crowned, and finally, the dance.

I can't wait for the game because I'm dying to see if Alex is going to win. He didn't even want to run but we all convinced him to sign up. I spent hours making posters for him, putting them up all over school, and passing out rally tags to everyone I know. He's going to win. I know it.

I sure as hell don't want *Ben* to win.

Seriously...Ben made the King's court too. I guess it's one of the perks of going out with a cheerleader. Vanessa probably showed some boob to all the boys to get them to vote for Ben. Well, I don't really know that, but I wouldn't put it passed her. Ben probably wouldn't have cared either. Actually, what would I know...I haven't talked to Ben in such a long time. I see him at school and he gives me his smart ass smile or makes some rude comment to me or Eric. That guy is just a sore loser. He thought he could play me and it didn't work, not entirely.

As long as Ben doesn't win king, I'll be happy.

But if Alex wins, I'll be ecstatic!

I'm surprised to see Alex as I pack up my soccer stuff. Soccer is almost over and I can't wait to be free. I feel like my life has been taken over. It will be great to be able to go straight home after school and just veg out if I want. I can actually take a nap like most other teenagers or go to the mall or something.

"Hey Alex," I shout. "What are you doing here?"

He walks over to us and smiles, "Hi Keesha...Hey Megan, can I talk to you when you're done?"

"Uh...sure, give me a sec," I respond. He walks away and I look at Keesha, confused.

"What's that about?" she asks.

"I have no idea," I mutter.

I quickly throw all my crap in my bag, put a piece of gum in my mouth, and slip on my flip-flops. "I'll be right back," I tell Keesh.

As I walk over to Alex, I'm nervous. This is totally out of the blue. He's never met me at my soccer practice before. He's been to my games, but with the rest of our friends too. We talk all the time, on the phone, email, texting...but this, is not normal. What does he want?

"So wassup Alex." I say, nervously. I smile. "What are you doing here?"

"I need to ask you something." He starts. "But I wanted to ask you in person, and not in front of everyone else."

"Oookaaay."

"The rally is next week and I have to have an escort to walk me on stage, right...so I asked Amy...but...but...but I'd like to know if you will be my escort too?"

My mouth drops open. I'm standing here in shock. Did I just hear correctly? Do I need to clean out my ears? Did I get hit in the head with the soccer ball today?

Seriously...is he crazy?

"You've done so much for me, I probably wouldn't have even run or made court without you. This is my way of saying thank you. So, what do you think?" he asks.

I'm still in shock. I need to gather my thoughts before I can answer. "Hmm...you don't need to thank me...it was fun, like being a campaign manager, or something. Don't you think it's kind of weird to have two escorts? What did Amy say?" I'm full of questions.

"Uh...people have two escorts all the time. Anyway, it doesn't matter. I want you to do it," he answers.

"And Amy?" I wait.

"I haven't told her yet. I wanted to see what you'd say first. But trust me, it'll be okay." He smiles.

That smile can get me to do anything. His big brown eyes stare down on me and I melt. This boy is a dream. I can't help but be mesmerized by his sweetness, his big eyes, his beautiful full lips, moist and kissable, his gorgeous smile...

"Sure...it sounds like fun!" I screech. "If it's okay with Amy, it's okay with me!"

"Cool Meg!" He throws his arms around me and flings me off the ground and spins me around.

OMG! I have never felt these arms before. I just sink into his hug and enjoy the moment. That tingling sensation I felt that one time in the car, is back and it pierces my body from head to toe.

"Ahemmm…"

Alex stops suddenly and we turn to see Eric and Keesha standing there. Eric looks me in the eye, then down at my feet dangling in the air.

Alex puts me down and croaks, "Hey 'sup Eric?"

"Not much…just came to pick up my girl," Eric says, standoffish. "Wassup with you?" His eyes are shooting daggers at Alex right now. If looks could kill….

"Just came by to talk to Meg about something, but I've gotta go now," he says. "Meg, I'll talk to you later…after I talk to Ames, okay?"

"Yeah…yeah…sounds…good," I stutter.

"See ya later," he says to us all and walks away quickly. Maybe he is as uncomfortable as I am right now.

"Late," Keesha says.

I take my bag from Keesha and start walking as well. "Let's go," I tell Keesh and Eric.

After a few steps, Eric asks, "What was that all about?"

"Oh." I hesitate. "Alex just came by to talk to me about the rally. He wanted to see if I'd be his escort." I don't have to wait long to see the wild expression on both their faces.

"What?" Eric shouts. "Isn't his girlfriend supposed to escort him? What the hell Meg?" I don't think I've ever heard him raise his voice…till now.

He sounds angry. I've never even seen Eric angry before. He doesn't need to say anything else. The fury in his eyes is saying it all.

"What are you trippin' for Eric?" I try to calm him, holding his hand. "Amy *is* gonna escort him. He just asked me too, as a kinda 'thank you' for helping him with his campaign."

"Amy is gonna flip," Keesha blurts. She begins to chuckle and shake her head. I think she's enjoying this too much.

"Why?" I ask, trying to sound innocent. Isn't this innocent?

Keesha stops suddenly and stares at me. "Uhh…never mind," she says and continues walking, gesturing at Eric and letting me know we'd save this conversation for later.

Eric is just silent. I can see the wheels turning in his head, but he still doesn't say anything. He doesn't have to. Now, his ears are lava red, his nose is flared, his breathing is intense. I look up at him and his eyes bare down on me like the Sun.

Maybe this isn't such a good idea after all.

The rally is awesome! The theme is "America's Best Dance Crew" You can imagine how excited Keesh and I are since that's our favorite show. Alex's skit is off the hook. He does this dance with all the football guys like the *Jabbawockeez* with masks and gloves, and everything. Who knew these big beefy guys could dance? It is awesome.

Ben's skit is supposed to be like *Step Up 2 To The Streets*— you know, their dance at the end of the movie. Ben does the whole *Moose* thing, and he does it well. Damn...he looks hot even. That part sucks but I can be mature and admit his skit is good...and he looks good.

The other guys are alright. One guy does Grease Lightening, another does a West Side Story dance, and the last guys does some swing dance thing. I don't know them well, so I don't pay much attention. Plus, it's hard to see everything from backstage. Yes...backstage...remember? Amy and I escorted Alex. She seems to be okay with it. Everyone was worried, including myself, but what is the big deal...Alex and I are just good friends.

The best part of the whole Backwards thing is the Powder Puff Game. The girls play flag football with ferocity, like animals. The senior girls play against the juniors and both teams are out to get blood. They're supposed to be playing for fun but they block like they're in the Super Bowl. The boy cheerleaders are hilarious—most in wigs and drag make-up, and fake boobs. I think some of them actually shaved their legs. It's hysterical!

At halftime, I'm going crazy with impatience. The show isn't too long. The mascot does this little dance and then Mr. Mitchell takes the mic.

"And now what you've all been waiting for...the crowning of this year's Backwards King!" Mr. Mitchell announces like a professional.

The Bengal Mascot runs around all the Backwards Princes. He stops at one guy, then runs back to stand in front of Ben. Oh No! Then, goes to the other dude, circles the other guy, before stopping in front of Alex Aguilar to hand over the crown. I scream till I can't scream anymore. Even Keesh and Steph are jumping up and down. The guys clap and whistle, but not with as much craziness as us girls. Amy's on the field so she runs up to Alex to congratulate him. It's cute, really.

Alex won!

Alex is the King!

After the game is over, we all crowd on the field. It takes forever, but we finally make it to Alex to congratulate him. It just so happens Ben is there as well. I didn't realize Alex is talking to Ben again.

"Damn Alex, you had it all figured out how to win," Ben chuckles. "It's genius really."

"Can you just shut up for once," Amy yells.

"What? Alex is brilliant. I wish I thought of it. I actually didn't even get it till I saw both of you on stage with him," Ben taunts.

"What the hell are you talking about now?" Alex shouts at him.

"Hmm...let's see. Hook up with a Freshman and it's like you're likely to win 'cause they have the biggest class and most of them vote. But when you're hooking up with one and you're in love with the other...shit, the win's guaranteed. Nice strategy, big guy!" Ben says intently, staring down Alex and shoving him in the arm.

Wham!

Amy slaps Ben right across the face and runs away from the crowd. Eric glares down at me, gives me a nasty look, and takes off too.

"You're such an asshole Ben!" I shout in his face.

"If it's not true, then why's Alex still here with you and not running after his girlfriend?" Ben yells back at me. He freakin' yells at me.

Alex lunges at Ben, but he moves out of the way too fast. Alex tries again, but before he can get to Ben, Steph jumps in the way.

"Alright, that's enough, you jerk...let's go Meg," Steph says.

She puts her arm around me, and with Keesha at my other side, we walk away.

"Uggh! I can't believe I ever actually liked that guy! He's such an ass! I hate him! I hate him!" I cry, trying to hold back tears.

"Meggie, don't even trip...let's just find Amy and Eric and go. Who gives a shit what that guy says anyway?" Keesha offers.

"Hey...wait up!" Alex yells, running to catch up with us.

We stop to wait for him.

"Meg, I'm sorry about Ben. He's just stupid sometimes. What the hell we gonna do? Amy and Eric looked pissed," he says, catching his breath.

I take out my phone to call Eric. I don't see him anywhere.

"Eric's not answering," I tell them.

Alex closes his phone. "Neither is Amy."

"Let's just go...we'll figure it out later," Keesh suggests.

"You guys wanna ride? Where you goin?" Alex asks.

"We're going to my house. We're all supposed to stay there tonight," I explain.

Alex drops us off at my house. Amy texts to say she went home but she won't pick up her phone to talk. Neither does Eric.

Tomorrow, this dance is going to suck!

Keesh, Steph, and I start getting ready for bed. We're pretty simple, so we just get into some big tees and soccer shorts, and brush our teeth. Keesh turns on the radio and sets the volume to barely audible. It's going to be a long night. We'll probably rehash the entire night, especially what Ben said. Maybe the girls can figure out a way to smooth things over with Amy and Eric.

My mind wanders to Alex—he is probably thinking about the same thing.

The girls tell me to just lay low and not say anything. They remind me Amy will speak to me when she's ready. But I don't know about Eric. This is unchartered territory for us. We've never had a fight before.

I'm starting to doze off when my phone startles me. It's a text.

"Who is it?" Keesh asks.

I flip my phone open to view the text.

"It's Alex, wants to know if I'm up," I whisper. Steph is snoring.

"Tell him I said hi and good night," Keesh says, as she yawns. She turns on her other side and goes back to sleep. I look at the time. It's pretty late.

I take a look at my friends sleeping next to me and at the foot of my bed. I prop up a pillow and lean against my headboard.

I text Alex.

Yup, I'm awake.

Within seconds, I get a text back. He's quick.

How u doin?

good...u?

ok

I type in the next one: **so what up?**

just wanted to say hi

I smile.

Hi!

I wait again.

g'night!

nite

dnt let the bd bugs bite

Oh my gosh, he remembers.

sweet dreams!

I smile.

merry xmas!

I giggle. I bet he's laughing too.
I text: **Happy New Year**
Happy hannukah.
I laugh out loud. Steph stirs in her sleep.
thats a new one...happy kwanza.
I'm giggling like a little kid, waiting to see what's next.
ooo that's a good 1
I try
ur funny Meg
g thnx I do wht I can...lol
anytime
lol...thnx ill be here all week...
okay g'night
nite
say gnite to the girls 4 me
k
bye Meg
bye alex

I text this whole time with a giddy smile on my face. I'm so lucky to have such a good friend. I imagine Alex sitting on his bed smiling, thinking about me and thinking the same thing.

25

"Hey babe!" Eric says over the phone. "So are we still meeting at your house?"

It takes me a second to register the fact that Eric's tone is friendly. I think for a moment and decide to double check I'm hearing him correctly. "Yeah, why wouldn't we be?"

"Uhh..uhh...I don't know," he stutters. "It's just things got a little crazy last night and I just wanted to make sure."

"Yeah, Ben's just a jerk," I say. "I don't even pay attention to his bullshit anymore. He's just a loser...give me a break...what is he jealous or something 'cause you and I are still together. He's got Vanessa...you would think he'd just stop with the crap already—he's just making himself look stupid. I just feel bad for Amy...I would hate for someone to say that you liked someone else...actually, I'd trust you," I pause. "Hey, did you see where Amy went last night?"

"Uhh...me...uhh...no!" Eric mumbles. "I...I just went home...I guess I got a little sick of Ben and just needed to clear my head."

"And...you good now?" I ask.

"Yeah...yeah, I'm a'ight," he says. "Hey, I've gotta go get ready, so I'll be over as soon as I'm done."

"Okay, bye."

I close my phone, thinking about Amy. She hasn't answered any of my calls. Steph and Keesh suggest we get ready and head to the dance as planned. They think she'll eventually show up either at my house or at the dance itself. I'm probably sweating over nothing, Amy welcomes drama.

By the time the guys all arrive, we're actually ready to go. My room is a disaster, make-up and hair products are scattered all over the place—hair spray, flat iron, curling iron, eye shadows, brushes...you name it, you can find it somewhere in here. But when the doors open, we look good. Damn good, if I do say so myself.

I love that this dance is casual—I feel so much better in jeans and a cute tee rather than a formal dress. The only one of us who likes being all girlied up in heels and a gown is Amy, but she'd still look just as good today as she did at Homecoming.

We all take pictures in my backyard next to our pool. My mom thinks the pool is the perfect backdrop. We take couples pics first. Eric puts his arms around me for our picture but his arms are loose, like we're brother and sister. Maybe he *is* still upset about last night. The rest of our friends join us for a ton of group shots.

Just when I think we're finished, I hear Amy yell, "Sorry, we're late...can we take a couple extra group shots?"

"Sure, get in there Amy...Alex," my mom shouts.

They drop their stuff and run over to get in the picture. I'm very happy, and relieved, to see them here. The guilt I feel about what Ben said in front of Amy—and Eric—runs deep and I don't want to be the cause of any strain in our friendship or either one of our relationships. I just want to be happy and I want Amy to be happy as well. Even though, I can't help but wonder if there is any truth in what Ben said.

Actually, I secretly hope there is.

I know. I'm a horrible friend...and a horrible girlfriend. But this is Alex.

My mom snaps a few more. "Now make silly faces."

"Just look normal than Jonathan," Keesh jokes. We all laugh. He grabs her and pretends to put her in a choke hold. "Hey, watch my hair."

"Okay, I think I got enough," my mom says to us with a chuckle.

I skip over to my mom. "Thanks!" I give her a hug and say goodbye.

We walk over to school for the dance as planned. Even Amy and Alex walk with us even though they can drive there. I'm sure it is Alex's idea because Amy would never wanted to exert any unnecessary energy. She might break a sweat if we walk too fast or her make-up might melt in the sun. Sometimes I think I'm a little hard on her, but then she does something to prove me right.

The guys walk ahead together, talking guy stuff and acting like little kids. Anyone can tell the difference between the three immature freshmen and the one senior. The younger guys goof around while they walk, smacking each other in the back of the head, pushing each other into one another, and talking about which girls are hot. Josh and Jonathan brag about the latest chicks they hooked up with and give each other knuckles, nugs, pounds, whatever you want to call it. Alex just smiles and laughs here and there but is a lot calmer than the others. Maybe this isn't normal behavior for older guys...maybe Alex is just mature.

Keesha starts talking about how she can't wait to get to the dance to get her *swang* on. That leads to a discussion of the rally and how hot all the guys looked, and how well they danced, even Ben. Ugh! Unfortunately, the topic of last night's game invades our conversation.

"Amy...what happened to you last night anyway," Steph screeches. "We were worried!"

"I texted you guys," Amy states.

"I hope you didn't let that dumb ass Ben get to you...he's an idiot, so forget about him," Keesha snaps.

"Yeah...I'm over it...I just want to have some fun tonight," Amy exclaims.

I don't say anything. I just keep walking and listen. I'm not about to open my mouth and say the wrong thing. I'm fine just being an innocent bystander right now.

When we get to the dance, tons of people are already there. The cafeteria is decorated like a club scene. There are tall round tables everywhere, without chairs so we all have to stand. The multi-colored spinning lights and the strobe light make it hard to see much else other than the pulsing bodies already on the dance floor.

We find one empty table and throw our things down. Steph says she'll stay behind and watch our stuff while we go dance. We decide to take turns relieving each other at the table so none of our crap gets stolen.

Dancing is the same as usual...just like any party we've been to—well, without the drinks. The last party we went to a couple of weeks ago, Amy got so wasted I was sure she used her lunch, but she assured me she didn't. I drank too but made sure I didn't get out of hand because I'm not sure I'd be able to stand my ground with beer goggles on. Eric would probably end up getting lucky. He kept trying to give me another beer, but I kept saying no.

We all take a break at the same time to get something to hydrate ourselves. We're all sweaty and gross, and we weren't even dancing that long. I pull my hair back to get some air and can feel the moisture on the back of my neck. My face is itchy from the sweat mixing with my make-up. I knew I shouldn't have worn any. I never wear this much, but when you get ready with the girls, anything can happen.

The guys go to get us some drinks and cookies. Yes...I said cookies. Without all the grinding bodies, it would look like snack time in preschool. This "club" serves sodas and cookies. Whatever, it's better than nothing.

"Alex, Mr. Mitchell is looking for you...he said to go up front where the D.J. is," one of the ASB officers tells Alex.

Alex shrugs his shoulders, gives Amy a quick peck on the lips, and slithers his way through the crowd.

Just moments later, Keesh yells, "I love this song...let's go dance!" I've barely had enough time to take a swig of my water but I go anyway. We follow the path she makes to the dance floor. Eric stays back this time.

We all jam as *The Anthem* blares through the speakers. That song is hot. If you dance the whole song, I swear you can probably burn a thousand calories.

When the song finishes, Mr. Mitchell takes the mic, "Heeelllllooooooo Carver Bengals! Welcome to the King's Ball!" We all cheer and clap. Mr. Mitchell looks insane. He is decked out like a Jabbawockee, only he has his face painted instead of a mask, and big thick dreads are hanging from his hat. This is not out of character for him—he dresses in tiger print pants and a tutu for all the rallies.

He introduces all the princes one by one, and finally announces the King...Alex...King Alex, at last. *Bleeding Love* screams through the cafeteria, and Alex comes running over.

"Where's Amy?" he shouts.

We look around. She was just here a minute ago...while we were dancing.

"I don't know...maybe the bathroom...want me to go get her," Steph asks.

"Oh shit...there's no time," he says, hurriedly. "I'm supposed to be dancing right now."

We all look at the dance floor and the rest of the guys are out there with their girlfriends or dates.

"Meg, I know I probably sound like an ass...but will you dance with me?" he asks in despair.

"Uh...I don't think I should," I say, looking back for Eric. Where's Eric? He isn't at the table anymore.

"Meg, go on...Alex is gonna look *whack* if he's not out there," Josh yells at me.

I look from Keesha to Steph.

"Go Meg!" Steph pushes me toward him.

I take Alex's hand and he pulls me into the center of the dance floor.

What the hell is going on here? Where's Amy? Where's Eric?

They're going to die if they see us right now. That's it...I *am* the worst friend and girlfriend in the world.

We dance at a good distance from each other. I keep looking everywhere hoping I won't see Amy and Eric watching us. And I don't. Before the song finishes, I have relaxed in Alex's arms. I look into his eyes and smile. He smiles back and I feel something weird between us. Something different. Something new. I feel...hope!

It *is* hope.

In that instant, all my feelings from the summer come back. All those feelings and more—it isn't just an obsession with this older guy and his hot body, it's more than that. It's the realization that this guy who has become one of my best friends, can maybe become more than that. Not right now, of course...but maybe...someday.

The song finishes, everyone cheers, and they begin to crowd in as a new song starts. Alex doesn't let me go right away. He hugs me tight and whispers into my ear, "Thank you Megan...you're a good friend." He kisses me on my cheek and pulls away to dance, with our friends who have now joined us.

We're all here...all but Eric and Amy.

26

Carver High has an awesome girls' basketball team. They're like undefeated and are expected to win CIF. ASB has been making tons of posters—congratulating the team and announcing upcoming games—and putting them up all over school. So when none of us can think of anything to do this Friday, we decide to show our support and make an appearance at the game. It will be a nice change to see a team win, unlike our sad football team.

Basketball fans are wild. This is my first game. Since their season is at the same time as soccer, I can never make it. I usually go home after practice or games, but now the season is over so I have some free time. The fans at soccer games are usually just parents—students rarely go to our games. But it seems like the whole school is here, along with teachers and parents. Huh...maybe it's because this is the final game for league champs.

The cheerleaders are fairly entertaining with all their stomping and cool cheers.

"We're heading for a basket, we're moving down the floor, we are the Bengals, and we know we're gonna score!" they chant and the fans follow along. It's like a freakin' sing along.

It's intense until the final minutes of the game when our girls pull ahead and end up beating the other team by 12 points.

We all charge out of the gym and into the quad. "So what next?" Steph shouts.

We're outside of the gym already, so Steph doesn't have to shout. But you know Steph.

"Hey, my mom is at another New Kids concert tonight and my dad is at a poker night," I explain. "So we can just kick back at my house, maybe light a fire again and just chill."

We all agree and begin the pilgrimage to my house. Everyone seems to be getting along pretty well, even after the dance, when I was sure Amy was going to be pissed with me. Amy and Eric missed the whole thing and were totally okay with me filling in. Amy had to go to the bathroom and didn't want to walk over to them in the dark by herself. Since Alex was busy, she asked Eric to go with her. Amy actually thanked me for dancing with Alex. She said she would have felt bad if he had to look like an idiot standing there by himself because of her.

The guys get the fire started and arrange all the chairs, while the girls grab some drinks and munchies. We raid my cupboards for anything salty, like chips, and sweet, like cookies. I'm surprised when we're able to find a bag of Doritos and Oreos. Now that soccer season is over, my mom stocks less junk since I'm not exercising as much. My mom hates that my full figure is less than desirable. I don't really care, and neither does Eric, so why should she? Thankfully, my dad loves junk food so my mom still stashes some good stuff in the pantry for him every now and then.

We take the stuff out back and get settled. I plop myself next to Eric and he moves around until we fit comfortably together.

"So what are we gonna do during spring break?" I ask, trying to start up conversation.

"You guys know I'm gonna be gone the whole week," Steph exclaims.

"What...where you going?" Dominic asks. Dominic is one of Alex's friends and Steph's new *friend*. It was only a matter of time before Alex's friends infiltrated our group. I think it would've happened sooner if it wasn't for Ben turning out to be such an ass, and disappointment.

"Oh shit!" Steph covers her mouth to finish her chocolate chip cookie. "I guess I forgot to tell you. My family goes to Glamis every year so I'll be gone the whole week!"

"Glamis...do you ride?" Dominic says, surprised and interested.

Keesh chuckles. "That's like asking Steph if she breathes."

"Well...excuse me...but Steph and I don't know everything about each other, *yet*," Dominic responds, emphasizing the word *yet*, as he pulls her into his lap. She screams and kicks as he tickles her.

They're totally cute together. Ever since they met at the dance, they've been inseparable. Dominic is this big huge guy with wild curly hair. He is junior at Carver who plays the offensive line. He is giant, really—he makes Steph look as small as Amy. Had she sat in Eric's lap, she would've crushed him, but Dominic holds her like a little puppy.

"So what do you ride, hon?" Dominic asks Steph.

"A Banshee!" she exclaims. "Just call me *Ricky Bobby*, I like to drive fast."

What a retard! Steph is quoting a movie—*Talladega Nights*—but Dominic thinks it's hilarious. He lets out a huge laugh, then says, "If you ain't first, you're last."

OMG! These two are perfect for each other.

We all just watch them and smile, everyone except Josh. "So do you ride too, Dominic?" he asks.

Dominic stops tickling Steph long enough to answer, "Yeah, my family has been going down to Glamis for years. I ride bikes, and quads. My dad just got a rail to take my little brothers out. My mom doesn't want them to ride on their own yet."

"How cool...maybe we'll see each other up there some time," Steph gushes.

"Yeah...like spring break 'cause that's what I'm doing too!" He tickles her again.

"Yeah...cool," I hear Josh mutter under his breath—looks like someone's *jealous*. I can understand his misery though. This is the first time Steph has brought any of her friends around the whole group. Any guys she went out with besides Josh were usually on the down low. It's stupid really, because they were never really a couple couple, so who cares?

"Anyone else skipping town?" Keesh asks.

"Nah...I'll be around," Jonathan says.

"Me too," I add.

"I'm not going anywhere," Eric tell us.

"Not me," Alex says.

Amy and Josh both add, "Me either."

"So what are we gonna do then?" I ask.

"How about the beach?" Alex suggests.

"That sounds awesome," Amy tells him. "I love the beach!"

That sounds like ass to me! I HATE the beach! The thought of getting into a bathing suit in front of Eric or Alex or anyone else makes me want to throw up. Seriously...someone change the subject. Amy knows I hate the beach. Who wants sand all up in their crack anyway? I swear, every time I've been to the beach I come home with my own collection of sand that's probably still in my carpet to this day. I probably have tiny grains still stuck in my hair.

Ugh!

Not the *beach*!

"That's cool with me," Eric agrees. "There's this train thing we can take that goes down to San Clemente...that would be cool instead of just going to Newport."

"Yeah, I've heard about that...the girls down there are supposed to be hot too," Jonathan adds. Josh leans over to smack his hand.

"So we'll go to the beach one of the days," Keesh agrees. "What about the rest of the week?"

"I hear there's gonna be some fresh parties on the weekend," Dominic tells us.

"Yeah...I heard that too," Alex says, in between eating chips.

I take a big swig of my Diet Coke, and burp. Seriously...I just burped. Out loud. For everyone to hear! OMG! I can't believe I just did that. It just came out!

"Damn girl." Keesh laughs. "That was a good one!"

"That was sick Meg!" Eric pushes me away. I can't tell if he is serious or kidding.

Dominic burps too. It makes mine sound like a squeak. I laugh, my face burning with embarrassment. Everyone starts to laugh.

Then Steph burps too. She looks at me and nods. She's got my back. Dominic high-fives her. It isn't long before everyone is chugging their sodas and trying to out-burp one another. What a good guy Dominic is...he saved me. Eric and Amy look annoyed. They don't join our contest. For a minute, we sound like a chorus of burps.

We continue our night talking, laughing, stuffing our faces, burping here and there, which starts an upheaval of laughter each time. We decide to just see what comes up during spring break, but going to the beach is inevitable. Ugh!

By the time the fire goes out, it's late, and everyone decides to go home. Eric stays behind to help me clean up. I'm afraid of what being alone will mean to him, but he just kisses me good night. It's a nice kiss, not at all a 'let me rip off your clothes right now' kinda kiss like they have been lately. I guess he's finally given up on his goal to introduce me to womanhood. He even stopped bringing up ways to get me alone or trying to get me to talk about sex. I don't know what changed his mind, but I'm glad that it did.

I go to bed thinking about spring break.

It isn't for another two weeks. Maybe I can drop a size or two by then.

I get out of bed and hit the floor to do some sit-ups and push-ups. That's it! Diet starts tomorrow—nothing but salads and water.

I'm not about to let my fat hang out all over the place. A lot of girls at school don't mind showing off their *muffin tops*, but I'm not one of them. I don't get how some girls squeeze themselves into a size seven or nine, when they're clearly a thirteen or fifteen. I don't even get the girls that are a size five or seven and try to get into a one or three. They just make themselves look fat when they're really skinny. Since when did fat hanging over the side of your jeans become a fashion statement? I'm not about to go there.

Why can't we go somewhere else? For the love of God, why do we have to go to the beach?

OMG!

Kill me now...seriously...kill me now!

I HATE the beach!

27

Today we're going to the stupid beach…seriously…the FREAKIN' beach! My friends must hate me! The only one who agrees with me about how crappy the beach is Steph, but she's down in Glamis riding away on her dang quad. Turns out, Dominic's parents know her's and they're going to meet up down there, so they get to spend the whole dang break together. At least, she'll probably end up with sand in her crack, *too*, from the dunes.

I hate my friends for dragging me to the beach. I hope they all come home with a rash in their asses from sand burn! Did I mention, I HATE the beach!

Actually, I hope Ms. Gelson gets a rash. Can you believe she actually assigned us a novel to read during break? We have to read *To Kill a Mockingbird*. That totally sucks! I'm going to have to *Spark Note* this one. There is no way I'm going to spend my break reading some stupid old book. Seriously…why can't we read stuff that's interesting? Books with characters that talk and act like people in this decade, or even this century. My dad says *To Kill a Mockingbird* is a great book. He said he hated it when he read it in high school, but grew to love it as an adult.

It's one of his favorites.

Then why are we reading it now? I'm barely in high school. I'm not an adult yet.

Why can't we read authors that are still breathing? Like Laurie Halse Anderson, or Walter Dean Myers, Jerry Spinelli, or Stephenie Meyer. I would cry out in happiness if any teacher in my lifetime assigned *Twilight*. I can just picture it…Team Edward and Team Jacob debates. Team Edward would win, of course! We could totally read the whole series in a year. Seriously...they should change the freshmen English curriculum to include one *Twilight* book a quarter. Even the guys would like it...and I bet students would actually read, *for once*!

We decide to head to Huntington Beach instead of San Clemente like Eric had mentioned. The train thing ended up being way too complicated. Besides, the guys want a fire pit to roast hot dogs and marshmallows. This is apparently going to be an all day thing. Ugh! Why can't we just go at night?

The drive doesn't take long—less than an hour. Alex borrowed his mom's minivan so we could all go together. Some of his friends are going to meet us there. I bet he's getting sick of hanging out with a bunch of freshmen.

Finding a parking spot seems like an impossible task. I have my fingers crossed, in hopes that we can't find one, but like usual, my luck sucks. My bad attitude about the beach must show because Eric asks me what's wrong the whole way down. Like any girl, I say, "Nothing, I'm fine!"

I swear my feet feel like they're getting first degree burns as soon as they hit the sand. I drop my bag and jump around till I can get my flip flops back on.

Everyone just laughs. Josh actually drops his stuff and points at me, while he laughs hysterically. It isn't that funny! Alex passes by me saying, "Hey Meg, don't you pay attention in science...land heats faster and *hotter* than water." What a freakin' nerd! Does he think he's funny?

"Haha...I must have missed that worksheet," I scoff.

"We were probably at the Steel Grill, Meggie," Keesh laughs, shaking her head.

I can't help but let out a little chuckle. I probably look like a dumb ass.

Eric turns around and comes back to help me with my bags. He throws them over his shoulder and manages to hold both our chairs. All I have now is my back pack. Wow! Chivalry is not dead.

We catch up with our friends who have already claimed an unused fire pit. We start to set up all our stuff. I feel like a family—we brought a cooler, blankets, an EZ-Up shade, chairs, and tons of food. I feel all grown up. As much as I hate—seriously hate—the beach, I'm really grateful to have such cool friends, but not grateful enough to enjoy myself.

Eric takes off his shirt and tosses me the sunscreen, "Can you put some sunscreen on my shoulders and my back, babe?" Sand flies toward me with the bottle and gets into my eyes.

"Yeah, whatever," I say, as I get up from my chair. I slap the lotion on his back and barely rub it all in. He looks diseased with white splotches of gunk all over his back. Most girls would've taken advantage of giving a hot guy a rub down, but not me. Being at the beach brings out the worst in me—the closer everyone gets to stripping down to their bathing suits and getting into the water, the pissier I get.

"You want me to do you?" Eric asks.

"Excuse me?" I yell at him.

"Babe, chill...I'm taking about the sunscreen," he yells back.

"Oh...no, I'm good," I say.

"You're not gonna get in?" He stands, peering down at me, with his hands on his hips.

"No...not right now, you go ahead!" I exclaim.

He looks at me with annoyance, grabs his boogie board, and takes off toward the water. Josh and Jonathan follow not too far behind.

Keesh glides toward me in her one-piece bathing suit. Even though it's a one-piece, it's still sexy as hell. The sides are cut out and she's showing a lot of cleavage, a lot!

"You ready to go in?" she asks. Why is everyone in such a hurry to get into the water? Do they know fish eat, shit, kill, have sex, and give birth in that water? How freakin' gross? We may as well bathe in sewer water if we're so willing to go swimming in this nasty ass ocean.

"No...frick...I'll go when I feel like it," I yell at her, looking up with my hand shielding my eyes from the sun. I lean back to get comfortable in my chair.

"Damn, Meg...what's your problem?" She stands directly over me.

"I'm sorry Keesh," I apologize, then in a softer voice say, "you know I'm not the most comfortable person in a bathing suit." I begin to search through my backpack for a magazine.

"Don't give me that." She grabs my hand. "Come on, stand up." She pulls me to my feet. "Now, take off your shirt," she orders.

"What...nooo!" I cry. "Are you kidding me?"

"Come on...I know you have your suit on under there."

She waits. I wait. She isn't going to back down. Ugh! What a brat! I whip off my shirt.

"You look great, Meg...nice cleavage," she says, checking me out. "Now, wait here." She runs over to her bag and comes back with her shorts on. "Now, you don't have to take off your shorts...you'll be more comfortable."

I look at my friend and smile. I can't believe just months earlier I thought I'd never talk to her again. "Thank you Keesh," I hug her tightly. "You're the best."

Even though the ocean grosses me out, I still walk down and get in the water. I can't just leave Keesh hangin' after what she did for me.

We're splashing around, soaking in the sun when I notice Amy...ALL of her, from head to toe. She looks like a cover model for a swimsuit edition of *Sports Illustrated*. She has on a red two-piece bathing suit—a triangle top, that barely covers her nipples, with bottoms that tie on the sides so that her hips are almost bare. Did her mother really buy her that suit? Isn't it against the law for a fifteen year old to be out in public like that? Seriously...she is practically naked!

I'm not sure if I'm embarrassed for her...or jealous of her perfect body. And I can't imagine how Alex feels. All the guys within fifty feet of us are staring at her, even the old men with families. Alex has to feel either really proud or really pissed. I know I wouldn't want everyone staring at my girlfriend.

"You getting out already?" Amy asks, as I pass her and Alex.

"Yeah...just for awhile...I forgot to put on sunscreen," I say, coming up with the first excuse I can think of.

I don't notice Keesh tagging along right behind me, "Me too," she says. I give her a weird look. "What...black people can burn too."

"Well, hurry and come back in," Alex says. His eyes don't even make it to my face.

Keesh and I look at each other with big grins, and start laughing.

"Was he just checking out your boobs?" Keesh blurts out.

I cross my arms, feeling a little self-conscious. "Seriously...I think he was."

We laugh again.

I throw on a tank top and plop myself down in one of the chairs. Keesh tosses me a water bottle and we just kick back and relax, watching our friends. I'm annoyed because I can already feel the stickiness of the ocean water stuck to my body and the sand paper grit chaffing my skin. I can't believe people enjoy this shit!

I don't plan on getting back in that disgusting water. People watching and reading magazines sounds much better.

"Meg...Meggieeeeeeeeee." I hear a yell.

I hear my name faintly, a few times before I realize it's Amy.

I pull down my sunglasses to get a good look at her. "What?" I shout back.

She is waving at me, shouting, "Come here...Meggieee, C'mere!" What is she whining about? She never calls me that.

"What the hell does she want?" I ask Keesh.

She looks back at her magazine. "I don't know...just ignore her...she's probably fake drowning or something so that hot lifeguard will have to save her."

"I can't just ignore her." I throw down my magazines and walk out toward the water.

She motions for me. "Meg, come here!"

"What the hell Amy? I don't wanna go in the water," I tell her.

"Meg...Meg," she stutters. "I lost my bottoms."

"What?" I understand what she said, but need to hear it again...louder. I know, I'm evil.

"I lost my freakin' bathing suit bottom," she yells. "Now, go get me some shorts!"

"What do you mean you lost them?" I ask even though I know perfectly well what she means.

"Damn it Meg," she yells. "I'm naked here. Get me some freakin' shorts!"

By this time, all the boys hear what is going on. They're cracking up. Jonathan sounds like he's going to choke, he's laughing so hard.

"Don't you even dare come this way or I'll kick your ass!" She threatens them.

I wade out into the filthy water and take her some shorts. I pass them to her and yell, "That's what you get for wearing a Barbie-sized bathing suit on your big ass."

I slosh back up to our camp, leaving her behind.

Maybe next time she'll get a bathing suit that fits. But I doubt it.

The one thing I *can* handle about the beach is an evening bonfire. I love roasting marshmallows—but they have to be just right...barely melted and not burnt. Keesh brought her iPod and speakers, so we can dance and play around.

But my night is ruined. Some of Alex's friends show up. We've met most of them in passing and *most* of them are cool. The problem is that Ben is with them...and *he* is not cool. He brought Vanessa along, so maybe, just maybe, he won't act like a freakin' jerk for once.

Alex catches my eye, and shrugs his shoulders. "Meg, I'm sorry...I didn't think he would come."

"Don't trip...I'm good," I respond.

We all continue to go about our business. I can't let Ben consume me anymore. He's done enough already with his big mouth. I have to let it go.

Josh and Jonathan start a hot dog eating contest. It's pretty disgusting. They try to be like the professionals, soaking the bread in water first and forcing down the dogs, sometimes two at a time. When they finish, Josh flicks his head up for everyone to see he has a hot dog bun stuck up his nose. He looks real proud. He puts his index finger on the side of one of his nostrils and blows out hard, the bread flies out like a canon ball. Gross!

"That was bad ass Josh," Jonathan says as they slap hands. Jonathan still has pieces of hot dog on his face.

They give up after sucking down five—I don't think they even chewed. The contest gives us something to laugh about for awhile.

"Hey...it's pretty late already. The time went by too fast," Keesh informs us.

"Yeah...too fast! It's time to go already. Darn!" I murmur, sarcastically.

We begin gathering our things to pack up. Damn, we brought a lot of junk. It seems like a never ending task since we brought so much crap with us. When we're finally ready to go, we have to wait—Amy and Eric have disappeared.

"Where the hell did they go?" Keesh asks.

"Eric went to the bathroom like twenty minutes ago," I explain, annoyed that he's still not back. I'm so ready to blow this taco stand.

"What about Amy?" Josh asks, sounding annoyed as well. "Alex, call her cell...she's pretty stupid to go somewhere by herself at night."

Alex tries to call her cell but she doesn't answer.

"It's about *time*," Jonathan says, spotting Eric and Amy before any of the rest of us do.

"Where were you Ames?" Alex asks. "I tried to call you and you didn't answer."

"Oh...oh, my cell is in my bag...you packed it," she lies. What the hell is she up to? I can see her cell in her pocket. Is Alex blind? "I went to the bathroom with Eric. You were packing all the stuff and I really had to go."

"What the heck took you so long," I complain. "We've been waiting here forever."

Ben interrupts. "There was a...long line," he says, nodding his head at Eric and Amy. What the hell is that all about? I didn't realize he was here till he said something. Maybe my Ben Radar is finally going away.

"Whatever," Keesh yells. "Can we just go? I'm freakin' tired."

We concede and get in the van. Everyone is too tired to talk on the way home. We all pretty much fall asleep until Alex pulls off the freeway. There's something about getting off the freeway that can wake you up no matter how deeply you're sleeping. It's like an alarm clock, signally you to wake up because you're almost home.

I jump in the shower as soon as I get home. I need to wash away the ocean funk from my body and rid myself of sand...endless amounts of sand. I throw on something cozy to sleep in and jump into bed.

I fall asleep dreaming about Ben and everything that has happened with him throughout this school year: meeting him at the party, him telling me I had options other than Eric, the big reveal that he had a girlfriend, him talking crap about me choosing second best, the powder puff game—ugh...that one was bad—when he said that crap about me and Alex, and today, "there was a long line." But that doesn't mean anything. At least he didn't talk crap this time.

28

"Hey Mom, can I have everyone over tomorrow to swim and order pizza?" I ask her nicely, hugging her for an added touch. I really don't need to do anything to butter her up. My mom is pretty cool about letting me have friends over.

"That sounds like fun, but my book club meets tomorrow and it's my turn to host it."

"So what does that mean?" I question.

"Well, as long as you don't care if there is a house full of women, it's okay with me," she explains.

"No...I don't care." I admit, smiling. "Thanks mom, I'm gonna go call everyone."

I practically skip to my room and take out my cell. I start to call Eric first and shut my phone. Instead, I start texting everyone. This method is so much faster.

Pool Prty n Pza @ my house 2mro @ 2. Whos in?

Within seconds, all but Amy text back to let me know they'll be here. I know she'll come, she's just being Amy.

Most of us haven't gotten together since we went to the beach. I've spent some time with Eric. He came over to watch movies one night and we went out for ice cream on another. Things have been much better with us since he gave up on the sex thing. I'm enjoying being around him again. But not much else has happened. Spring break turned out to be pretty relaxing. I thought we were going to be going non-stop.

The weather is nice out—hot with a little breeze so it's tolerable. I was actually worried that it'd be chilly. When you think of Spring Break, you always think of sunshine, the beach, and crazy parties. But in reality, you never know what you're gonna get. Dang, that sounded very "Forest Gump." But I'm happy the weather is nice enough to be outside and swim— although, the guys are wild enough that they'd probably swim in a freakin' hail storm anyway.

Everyone arrives right on time. I set up some chips and fruit on a table outside. Since it's so hot, I figure some strawberries will be refreshing. My mom got us some bottles of water, Gatorade, and sodas. I also throw some extra towels outside just in case anyone forgets their own.

Jonathan and Josh are the first to jump in—with giant cannon balls that practically empty the pool. Eric and Alex follow them. Amy takes her time—I knew she'd show up—taking off her clothes to reveal her new bathing suit. Seriously...she is totally putting on a show, sliding her shorts off slowly, seductively down her hips inch by inch, over her knees, and bending over, holding it for a sec to take them off completely. She pulls off her shirt in the same way, and tosses her hair about as it comes over her head. It's like she did it in slow motion. Sad thing is, the guys are goofing around and don't even notice her charade. This time she wears a one-piece but it shows enough skin to be considered lingerie.

Keesh just watches the striptease with a glare. She yells, "Hey Amy, what happened to your red suit?" She laughs, and turns away, not even waiting for a response from her.

She says it loud enough for everyone to hear. Everyone chuckles until Amy flashes us a devilish look. She continues her show by slicking herself up in sun tan oil and lying down on her back to toast.

Keesh just flips off her clothes and sits in a chair next to her. No show...no oils...no flashy bathing suit. Keesha is wearing a regular normal-looking suit today. It's nice to see at least one of my friends still shows respect for their elders. Come on, does Amy really have to wear that in front of my parents?

Eric walks up dripping and gets a towel. He dries himself off a bit before saying, "Hey Meg, can we get some drinks?"

"Sure!" I jump up out of my chair. "Wanna help me get some?"

He follows me inside to find a table full of women…my mom's book club friends. Actually, they're all her college buddies, but they use the book club as a way to stay connected.

"Oh…hi ladies." I smile. "Nice to see you all again."

"Hi Megan," one of them says, looking from me to Eric.

"Oh…everyone, this is my boyfriend Eric." I gesture to Eric. "And Eric, this is Teri, Shazia, Sarah, Stephanie, Ellen, Andrea, Edita, and Sylvie." He shakes each one of their hands to greet them. He is so polite, it only makes him cuter.

"There's gonna be a test later," Sylvie jokes.

"Well, I'm sure I won't forget you," he winks at her. Is my boyfriend flirting with one of my mom's friends?

"Come on." I push him into the kitchen. "See ya later ladies."

We get out of earshot before Eric says, "Damn, those ladies are fine. I expected to see a bunch of old women with gray hair or something. Your mom's got some hot friends."

"Chill Eric, don't get too excited." I punch him in the arm. "Were you seriously flirting back there?"

He just laughs and kisses me on the cheek. We grab the drinks and stroll outside. The rest of the guys have gotten out of the pool. Josh jogs over to Keesh and Amy before shaking out his hair and body, like a shaggy dog, trying to get them wet. Keesh thinks it's funny but Amy shoots him one of her evil glares.

"You guys gotta go in there and check out Meg's mom's friends." Oh my gosh…he's still on this kick. "There has to be like ten MILF's in there right now."

I stop him. "Calm down Stiffler before I punch you again."

The boys laugh and Amy asks, "Who's Stiffler and what's a MILF?"

"Oh my God, Amy…you're whack," Josh laughs at her.

Alex asks, surprised, "Haven't you ever seen any of the American Pie movies?"

She shakes her head. Where in the hell has she been?

Keesh giggles. "Stiffler's like this sex crazed idiot who never gets any and a MILF is a...," she holds up her fingers to make quotes, "mother I'd like to...you know...use your imagination," she explains.

The boys laugh hysterically, slapping hands, thrusting their hips, making humping gestures. Even Alex joins in this demonstration which makes it even funnier.

"You guys are sick." I punch Eric again, this time in the gut, and push Josh on my way to the pool. I would have socked them all if they were in reach. I take off my shirt, leave my shorts on, and sit at the edge of the pool with my feet in the water. Keesh and Amy stay put in their chairs, while the guys keep getting in and out of the water, taking turns going inside to get a look at the MILFs. Jerks!

I get sick of sitting there by myself. There are only so many crazy dives the guys can do before they all look the same. Boring. I get up and walk over to convince Keesh to keep me company.

"You know I just think it's a little too much of a coincidence, Amy." I hear Keesh say as I get closer.

"What's a coincidence?" I ask them both.

"Uhh...nothing." Keesh looks startled. She gets up and walks toward the pool. "I was just gonna go sit with you."

"Oh...okay." I follow Keesh back to the water. Uh-oh...what did Amy do to piss off Keesh now?

"Heeeyyyy...I'm heeeere so let the partaaaay begin!" I know that voice anywhere. I turn my head quickly to see Dominic stripping off his shirt, throwing it to the ground, and running to a flying leap into the pool. Well...I don't need to jump in the pool *now*. Dominic soaks both Keesh and I with his ginormous cannon ball. He was so quick—there wasn't anything we could do to get away.

We all start busting up laughing. It's hilarious—we must look like wet cats. It's a good thing Amy wasn't sitting with us 'cause she would've gone apeshit on his ass for getting her wet.

"What are you guys doing here?" I squeal. "I thought you weren't getting back till tomorrow."

"Our parents decided to leave early to beat the traffic...I called you but you didn't answer your cell so I called your house. Your mom told me you were all here, so we thought we'd surprise you...Surprise!" she yells.

"Cool!" Steph kicks off her flip flops and sits next to us. I ask, "So how did it go? Did you impress Dominic with your riding skills?"

"She means with your bike, Steph..." Keesh giggles, jokingly.

"Good one Keesh," Steph chuckles. "We had a good time. It was kind of weird being around our families, especially my dad. What dad wants to see some guy hugging on his daughter? But he was pretty cool. We rode all day, had campfires, and we went for walks at night. It was sooooo fun."

"So what did you do on those walks....huuuhh Steeephhhh?" Keesh pushes.

"We held hands, cuddled in the sand, and watched the stars," she says, all girly.

I try to picture it. "Ahhhh....how romantic!"

"That's a bunch of crap," Keesh tells her. "Dish all the dirty details...come on Steph."

"Dang Keesh, you're as bad as my boys over here," Dominic jokes, as he swims over.

"Yeah...and like you didn't spill your guts just now," she accuses.

"Nope...not a word," he stands up, gives Steph a quick peck, then settles with his back to her. She repositions herself to let him rest his back against her, with her arms over his shoulders and on his chest. He smiles and turns his head back to kiss her on the cheek. They're just so freakin' cute together.

I look for Eric, wanting to cuddle, of course, after seeing Dominic and Steph—but he is sitting down next to Amy on the deck. Seriously...are they like BFF's now or what? I stare at them for awhile, trying not to lose track of the conversation with everyone else. I notice that Alex is watching me stare at Amy and Eric.

He swims over to me. "So what's up, Meg?" Alex asks, wiping the water from his face.

"Since when did *your* girlfriend and *my* boyfriend become best friends?" I ask, only loud enough for him to hear.

We both watch Amy and Eric sunbathing next to one another. They aren't talking or anything, they're just there...together.

"It's no big deal," he shrugs. "*We* actually hang out and talk more than they do."

Yeah, but that is different, kinda. The more I think about Alex and I, the more I think I might have something to worry about with Amy and Eric. I mean...there is definitely a piece of my heart that still feels something for Alex. I won't act on it or even admit it out loud but the feeling is definitely still there. Eric is much too nice for Amy, though. Well...so is Alex.

Ugh! Who cares? I'm probably making something out of nothing.

There is a big unexpected splash. Amy and Eric just jumped in the water. Everyone else joins them but I'm fine sitting with my feet in the water.

"Hey, let's do a chicken fight," Keesh yells.

"Yeah...I bet Meg and I could whoop all your asses," Eric looks over at me, nodding his head.

"Nah...I'm good," I say, thinking I'd probably snap his neck trying to get my big ass on his shoulders. "I've gotta go to the restroom...you guys play without me."

I pull my feet out of the water and stand. I don't have to go to the restroom but I need to act the part. I go inside and watch them from the window. Keesh and Jonathan have Alex and Amy beat every time. Amy has a fierce attitude, but physically, she's weak—she probably doesn't want to screw up her manicure. When they finally settle down, I casually walk back outside.

"Wanna play now?" Eric asks as soon as he sees me.

"No thanks...I'm gonna work on my tan over here." I quickly make up an excuse.

I look around for Amy's suntan oil and see it peeking out of her bag. I go over to pull it out and see a brown paper bag. Is that *the* brown paper bag, her lunch? OMG! I look around and no one is watching so I open the bag.

OMG! Seriously...she's had lunch...like really *haaad* lunch.

Oh crap! She's having sex with Alex—no wonder he doesn't care about Eric, he *has* Amy...he is *having* Amy a lot by the looks of it. There are less than half the condoms that we started with. We both got the same amount and I know exactly how many I have and there is definitely some missing from Amy's bag.

I close Amy's lunch, her bag, and plop myself down in my chair. Thankfully, she doesn't notice me in her stuff. I spray the oil all over my body. I'm practically dripping by the time I realize what I'm doing. I stop spraying and try to rub in as much as possible. Screw it...I grab a towel and start wiping the shit off. I stop suddenly and just observe my friends in the pool. I study Amy and Alex.

Seriously...my best friend had sex with *Alex*.

I spring to my feet and make a mad dash for the flower bed.

There, I toss my cookies—I throw up my breakfast, my Gatorade, my chips, and I yak up...my heart.

29

I missed all the parties that last weekend of Spring Break. After puking my guts out at my own pool party, I can't show my face. Actually, I don't know if it's the fact that I vomited chewed up strawberries and chips in front of my friends or that I don't want to be around Amy and Alex. Seriously...I don't want to be around Eric either—I feel so guilty the whole sex thing bothers me so much. I can't believe I have a sweetheart for a boyfriend and I'm trippin' over some other guy. And not just any guy—my best friend's boyfriend.

Getting back to school is exactly what I need to take my mind off things. All the teachers are going nuts trying to cram in review before state testing. As if it matters, there are few students that pay attention to these stupid tests anyway.

Most of the time, we don't even find out how we score or what the scores really mean. My dad thinks it's a conspiracy. He believes politicians are making money off the testing companies, so as long as this high-stakes testing crap is around, the politicians will just get richer. It doesn't help that he's a math guy either. He's always going on about how not all kids can pass if they're scored on a bell curve. I get that part. Come on now, I'm in Algebra two. Any lamo can figure out that half of students have to score below average and half have to score above on a bell curve. I'm only in ninth grade for crying out loud, why can't the people who make up these dumb laws figure this out?

The only test I care about is the high school exit exam, but I don't have to take that till next year. Testing has even taken over

ASB—they have us sharpening pencils like crazy. I guess our school leaders are not aware of the fundamental rule of test taking: use a dull pencil. It takes less time to fill in the bubble that way.

In sixth period, Ms. Gelson lets us work with a partner to work on some study questions. Eric and I scoot our desks next to each other. This is a bad idea...we won't get anything done.

"What are you doing after school?" Eric asks.

I pretend to read a passage as Ms. Gelson walks by, "Nothing...wanna come over?"

"Yeah...I'll walk you home."

We stare at our papers but don't do anything. Eric sits with his knee bouncing up and down like he is nervous about something.

"Is everything okay?" I ask him, putting my hand on his leg. "What's up?" He is obviously worried about something.

"Uh...Meg...don't you think everything's a little different lately?" He looks down, pulling a piece of loose skin on his thumb.

Everything. Different. What exactly is he talking about?

"What do you mean? Can you be a little more specific please?" I'm worried now too.

Everyone looks over at us. I get closer to him so we can whisper.

"I'm talking about us. Things seem different lately...don't you think?" he says, crinkling the skin between his eyes, as if he's hurt.

"Yeah...I kinda know what you're talking about...it seems like we're more like friends than a couple," I explain. It's nice to get this off my chest.

"Yeah...that's it," he agrees.

"Is it because I'm not ready to have sex...'cause I think that's when things started to change?" I can't believe I asked that.

"No...come on, Meg. No!" he says, angrily.

"Don't act all surprised...after new year's, you couldn't stop talking about it...then all the sudden you just gave up...you don't even kiss me the same."

Ms. Gelson makes another round and we look down at our papers.

When she passes us, Eric snarls, "What and you weren't different...you've barely even touched me after that night...it's like I have a disease."

"So why didn't we just break up then?" I ask.

"I don't know...maybe we should've...but I kinda think our friends keep us together."

I finish his thought, "It's like we just act like a couple so it won't be weird with all our friends. Like a couple who doesn't get divorced for the sake of the kids...we go out and kiss and stuff, but it just isn't the same."

"Weird huh...now when we kiss, I feel weird...like I'm kissing my sister," he chuckles.

Some girls would've been pissed at that comment, but I'm okay with it.

"So what do we do then...I don't want to stop hanging out with you...or Josh...or Jonathan...and I don't think Keesh, Steph, or Amy would like that either. We created a little family here and I don't want to lose that." I tear up.

"No...I don't want to lose it either. I think I can still hang out. We can still be friends. We just won't have any other...privileges."

"You really think it will be okay?" I'm totally sniffling now. I'm surprised Ms. Gelson hasn't come over, or my girls.

He puts his arm around me and holds me tight. "Oh babe...don't cry...it'll work," he says, trying to comfort me.

I still cry. "I don't know why I'm crying...I know everything will work out...I'm totally okay with this...I just feel all sad...but I don't know why," I ramble.

"Meg, I'm sad too...I thought we were going to get married and shit...be like high school sweethearts, or whatever," he adds.

"Hey, I gotta go get some air." I step out of my seat and walk over to Ms. Gelson, with my hair in my face so my classmates can't see that I'm crying. I ask her if I can go to the restroom. One look at my puffy red eyes and she shoos me out of class.

I fling open the door and start to walk quickly down the hall. I don't get far before someone grabs my arm.

"Meg...what's wrong? What happened? Are you okay?" I try hard to focus through my tear-filled eyes to see who all these questions come from. It's...Ben.

"Oh shit, Ben...not now...leave me alone," I whine, trying to break free.

"Just tell me what happened. I'll let go when you tell me you're okay!" He looks at me frantically, with worry in his eyes.

"I'm fine alright...it's not like you freakin' care, so go away." I pull myself loose from his grip and start to walk away.

"Come on, Megan," Ben argues. "You know I do care about you."

I stop and turn to look at him, "Are you freakin' kidding me?" I pause for a moment trying to catch my breath. "You did nothing but play me at the beginning of the year. And then all you've done since is talk shit...oh, but yeah, you care about me!" I yell at him. It may have taken the whole school year, but right now, we are going to have it out. This has been coming for a *long* time.

He stares at me, his nose flaring, before he starts, "I played you...give me a break, you started talking to freakin' Eric when you knew I was into you. I didn't even start talking to Vanessa until after that. You made me look like an idiot walking out of sixth period everyday all cuddled up with that asshole."

"Give me a break...you think I'm stupid...I should have listened to Eric from the beginning and I would've never even thought twice about you...don't call him an asshole either...he's one of the nicest people I've ever known, unlike you!" I shout at him.

"Then why are you crying?" he asks.

I forgot I was crying.

"Because….because…we broke up just now," I exclaim.

"It's about time you got rid of that loser. Are you sad or relieved?" he questions.

I hadn't thought of that before. Know what? I think I'm relieved.

"He's not a loser," I say, sticking up for Eric.

"Whatever…I'm not gonna argue with you. I'm just glad you're done with him. You could do a lot better," he claims.

"Oh really…like with you…yeah right!" I smirk.

"No…I wish. Alex was right about me. I don't deserve you…but *he* does. You and Alex belong together." He smiles.

"Are you high?" I interrupt. "You're freakin' crazy. Did you forget he's with my best friend?"

"No…and he needs to get rid of that skank." He stops when he sees my expression. "Sorry but, you'll see someday. That friend of yours is *not* a very good friend."

It sounds like Ben is tossing out accusations, but I ignore him. I trusted him once and that didn't get me anywhere.

"Whatever, I've gotta go before Ms. Gelson calls security or something," I explain.

"Yeah, I've gotta go to." He pauses. He steps forward with his arm up, like he is going to hug me, but drops it and backs away. Good choice. It's too soon for that. "It was good talking to you. I wish we could be friends again."

I look into his big blue eyes and I realize I've missed him too. "Yeah…well, maybe we can work on that," I snap at him as I stomp off to class. I'm not going to be too nice to him, not yet anyway.

30

Is the entire school here, or what? It looks like Halloween in April with all the orange and black the fans are wearing. The school pride at Carver is amazing. Today is a big game for Josh—he's pitching against our school rival, the Creekside Coyotes. There is so much pressure on Josh to do well. I almost feel bad for him. He's only a freshmen and he's on varsity. Everyone treats him like freakin' royalty on the field. I can't believe it doesn't get to him. Seriously, I can't believe he even plays as well as everyone says he does. He's just so goofy when we all hang out, totally uncoordinated and awkward.

It's a good thing we get to the field early or we would've never gotten a seat. We're all here, the whole gang. It's cool between me and Eric. It's taken some time to get used to. Once in a while, we'll catch ourselves leaning in for a kiss goodnight just out of habit. We both laughed uncontrollably last week when we left sixth period holding hands. We didn't even realize it till Amy pointed it out. Now, it's just funny if stuff like that happens. It's a good thing we didn't have sex...or that might've happened accidentally too. Well...probably not!

"Damn...Josh looks good in his uniform," Keesh yells. "Looks like I went out with the wrong friend." She elbows Jonathan in the ribs.

"You can still have him if you want," Jonathan throws it right back to her. "We're not married!"

"As if that will ever happen!" She pokes him again. He throws his arms around her and hugs her closely. She looks up at him and plants a wet one on his lips. "You'll just have to do...maybe Josh can let you borrow his uniform," she jokes. He releases her from the hug but holds her hand in both of his.

Keesh and Jonathan are back together, again. Seriously...we really need to meet new people! I refuse to get back together with Eric out of convenience.

"Wassup y'all...did I miss anything yet?" Ben shouts as he makes his way up the bleachers.

"Josh struck out the first three batters, now we're up to bat...no outs," Alex informs him.

"Damn...he's bad ass!" Ben takes out some sunflower seeds and throws a handful in his mouth. He passes the bag around for anyone to take some.

It was weird at first—to have Ben around again—but we've all gotten used to it. He doesn't go out of his way to talk crap like he used to, he just blends in. Alex was worried at first. He called me when he heard that Ben and I had talked after Eric and I broke up. He wanted to make sure Ben was cool about it and didn't say anything to make me more upset. I assured him it was all good. Since then, Alex has been very overprotective of me when Ben is around.

"Woooohooooo...Yeah," everyone cheers and claps. One of our guys hit a double sending another player home. Cool! The score is one-nothing, in the bottom of the second. Josh still hasn't given up a hit.

"I'm thirsty," I announce. The sunflower seeds dried out my mouth. "I'll be right back, I'm gonna go to the snack bar...does anyone want anything?"

Ben stands up. "I need a drink...I'll go with you," he says, taking a step down.

"Yeah...I'm gonna get something too," Alex pops up and starts down the bleachers too. I catch Amy rolling her eyes behind his back.

I follow them down the bleachers and hear Ben scolding Alex, "You need to chill bro...it's not like I'm going to kidnap her."

"I don't know what you're talking about," Alex denies the accusation.

"Man, come on…you don't even let Meg out of your sight if I'm around," Ben argues.

"Excuse me guys," I interrupt. "Can you stop talking about me like I'm not here?"

"Who says we were talking about *you*?" Alex smirks and winks at me.

"Whatever," I sock him in the arm. "Just stop trippin'…both of you. I can take care of myself. If I need either one of you, I'll ask."

"Well, fine then," Alex smiles. "You can buy your own drink!"

"That's a start, Alex." I smile back.

"So what do you want to drink then?" he offers.

"Diet coke, please!"

"Alright Miss Independent," Ben chuckles. "That lasted like thirty seconds."

We just smile at each other, and I let out a small giggle.

The line is so long that by the time we get back, it's already the bottom of the fourth.

"Anyone hit off him yet," I ask.

Dominic has his eyes fixated on the game, but gives us the run down, "Not yet, he's been throwing hard, and his defense is backing him up. The Coyotes are going down."

"The Coyotes are going down…down, down, down," Keesh and Steph begin to cheer.

"Josh is up next," Eric says, as I sit down next to him.

The batter walks filling up the bases.

"Hey babe, what do you call it when you hit a homerun with bases loaded?" Steph asks.

"A grand slam!" we all shout.

"Damn…you don't have to yell," Steph yells back.

Everyone is to their feet, screaming and yelling, clapping and hollering.

"No…you retard. Josh…he just hit a grand slam!" I tell her shaking her with excitement.

"Holy shit! Oh shit! Alright Jooooosh!" Steph screams, as she stands up and stomps on the bleachers.

It takes the rest of the game to calm down from that excitement. Josh is amazing...he IS royalty! The game is so freakin' exciting, I almost pee my pants!

It's the top of the seventh, we only need three more outs and Josh makes history. Josh strikes out the first batter. The second batter pops up to the first baseman. And finally, the third batter hits the ball straight at Josh's head. I want to close my eyes 'cause I'm sure his brains are going to splatter all over the pitching mound. But no sooner than the ball is hit, Josh just puts up his glove and catches the ball. The sound is a big slap as the ball reaches his glove. Man, his hand is going to hurt. That had to sting! He makes it look so easy though, like it's just practice.

Game over.

Josh pitched a perfect no-hitter against our school rival, the Coyotes.

"The Coyotes went down...down, down, down," we all scream and yell.

We wait for the players to come out of the locker rooms.

We made signs in ASB saying, "Josh Rocks!" and "Josh is Our Hero!"—just in case we won and Josh did a good job.

We hold them up as he comes out and he is jumping up and down like a little kid.

I run up to him, and give him a big hug shouting, "You're freaking amazing!"

Everyone else does the same.

"You kicked ass!"

"You're bad ass!"

"Damn, that game was off the hook!"

For the rest of the night, it's all about Josh, as it should be. We go out for pizza and spend the evening talking about the game. We're like ESPN going through the highlights. It never gets old...we just kept talking away. Even all the girls join in the conversation. We're all delirious, drunk with happiness and envy.

There isn't anything in the world that could bring down this high...nothing at all.

31

The year is flying by and coming to a close. I can't believe in just a month, I'll be taking finals, and the school year will be over. I'll be a sophomore...we'll all be in tenth grade. All but Dominic, Ben, and Alex. Dominic will be a big bad senior. I'm not too sure what Ben and Alex are going to do. Wait...I can't believe we've never talked about it. I just assume they're going to college—that's what I'd be doing after high school—but really, I have no clue what their plans are. Maybe I've just never wanted to imagine high school without them, either of them.

Mr. Mitchell takes attendance and then gathers the committee chairs for a meeting. There isn't much to do so we all sit around talking. It's quickly interrupted by loud chatter and arguing coming from the meeting. I can't quite hear what is being said, but it sounds heated.

The doors fling open and they all come out. The guys seem to be relaxed, but the girls stomp out like they're throwing tantrums, as if someone just stole their MAC make-up or something.

Mr. Mitchell rings his bell, "Okay everyone, take a seat...I've got some announcements."

He waits for everyone to find a seat and be quiet. "Everyone needs to listen clearly...we've got some big decisions to make and the chairs thought it would be a good idea to bring it to a class vote...actually just the juniors and seniors will vote...but it affects everyone.

"We're having a problem with Prom. Ticket sales are down and as it stands right now, Prom may have to be canceled." Everyone gasps and there's an instant spark of chatter. "Okay, okay, quiet down...I'm not done yet. We have no interest in canceling Prom but we need to sell tickets.

"We have two options. The first option is to change the venue...we can change the location of Prom to the cafeteria to cut costs."

The girls groan. I doubt the guys care much.

"What's the other option?" someone shouts.

Mr. Mitchell continues, "Our second option is to open up Prom to freshmen and sophomores...wait, wait...let me finish/ Half of ASB includes underclassmen...we can limit the sales to ASB underclassmen first. If we still need to sell more tickets...we can open it up school wide. Now I'll take questions."

A senior girl argues, "I don't care who goes, I just don't want it in the cafeteria."

Another girl demands, "The only way I won't mind is if it's just the ninth and tenth graders from our class...I don't want it to be the whole school."

"Can we see how many of you would want to go," Mr. Mitchell gestures to us.

I look around and hands start to go up. I look at Keesh and she says, "Why not?" So we both raise our hands. Amy and Steph are already going so they don't really matter.

"By the looks of it, we could pull this off if everyone in the class bought a ticket, so let's take a vote," Mr. Mitchell explains. "On a piece of paper, write down cafeteria or underclassmen...when you're finished, give the paper to me...only juniors and seniors vote."

We wait patiently for the votes to be tallied before Mr. Mitchell announces, "Looks like the freshmen and sophomores are going to prom. You all need to find a date and buy your tickets by Friday. We'll reevaluate this plan at that time to determine if anything else needs to be done."

The bell rings and we all crowd through the hall to escape the classroom.

Our lunch crew is getting smaller. Amy is always with Alex and now Steph splits time between us and Dominic's friends. Keesh and I sit under the tree talking about Prom.

"So do you really wanna go?" I ask.

"Hell yeah...but I'll have to see if Jonathan wants to," she explains.

Jonathan strolls up just then. "So what do you want me to do?" He plops himself next to her and cracks open a smuggled Monster drink.

"Hey." She grabs his hand. "Wanna go to prom with me?"

"What...I thought only seniors and juniors can go to that."

"Not if you're in A...S...Beee!" I exclaim, with my hands in the air.

Eric and Josh join us. "Is it true that you guys can go to prom 'cause you're in ASB?" Eric asks.

"Yup," I answer.

"Need a date?" Eric asks me.

"Seriously...you'd wanna go," I question.

He chuckles, "Well yeah...what the hell else are we gonna do...all our friends will be there."

"Wait...Josh...are you going?" Keesh asks.

He blushes and mutters, "Yeah, I'm going."

Jonathan taunts him, "Mr. Big League here is going with Erica, the hot cheer captain."

Eric high-fives Josh while saying, "Damn...I think I need to change sports."

Keesh interrupts, "So I guess it's settled then, we're all going to Prom!"

"How freakin' cool!" I squeal.

What the hell was I thinking agreeing to go to prom? How could I forget what a pain in the ass it is to find a dress? I almost have a nervous breakdown before I settle on the same style dress as homecoming, but in a different color.

My prom dress is a burnt orange color. It looks great against my skin. The dress has black embroidered flowers at the bottom. It's actually quite beautiful, but as soon as I put it on, I feel totally uncomfortable and want to tear it off and throw on some soccer shorts and a t-shirt. Maybe I'm not supposed to be a girl.

My hair looks better this time too. The same guy did it, putting twists everywhere with curls coming down in precise places. He used about a million bobby pins. I would probably set off alarms at an airport. When I got home from Homecoming, my mom took all the pins out like a mama chimp eating the bugs off her baby. It took about a half hour to get them all out. This time it'll probably take an hour.

We all meet at Steph's house where a limo waits for us. When Eric and I arrive, everyone is already there—even Josh with his date and Ben with Vanessa. I really thought our older friends would ditch us today but they don't. I'm really surprised but it feels nice to know we all mean something to them. When I take a look around I realize Keesha and I are the only ones who aren't going with a junior or senior. Oh well...who cares!

When we walk up the red carpet at Prom, it feels like a fairy tale. There are doormen, not just one but two, who greet us by opening the double French doors and gesturing for us to pass through. They look real classy in black tailored suits with white gloves on. As we enter the room, it sparkles with twinkly lights and a giant chandelier. Round tables and chairs surround the dance floor. White linens cover each table and fresh flowers are arranged as centerpieces. The scent of the roses and freesia is intoxicating.

I have to remind myself to breathe. Every detail is perfect. No wonder the senior girls did not want to move the location. This is truly perfect.

We check our purses at the front desk so we don't have to worry about leaving someone at the table to guard our things.

We find two empty tables and take a seat—there are too many of us to fit at one. Servers come around and ask us what we want to drink, and place appetizers at our table. This is totally high class. I feel like Cinderella at a ball, excited to be here but a little out of place.

The music kicks up as the tables fill. The principal welcomes everyone and then it's time to get down. Unk's *Walk It Out* sends everyone crowding to the dance floor. Keesh, Steph, and I go wild. I'm one of the few girls who can really walk it out because my dress isn't skin tight. I don't have to worry about ripping my seam if I get too freaky. Well...neither do Keesh or Steph, but Amy...that's a whole other story.

The sweat starts to gather down my back and I can feel the moisture on my upper lip. The dance floor is so packed we could be standing still and we'd still be sweating. When a slow song finally comes on, Eric and I bolt for our seats.

I pick up my cloth napkin and pat my face. He starts to loosen his tie and take it off. He doesn't waste any time untucking his shirt and unbuttoning the top buttons.

"Damn Eric, I'm jealous...I'd like to take off this and that and get comfy," I cry.

"Well...you'd probably get us kicked out if you took off your dress," he jokes.

We make small talk till the fast songs return. This time Soulja Boy comes on and I can't wait to get out there to do the Superman. Keesh and I watched the video online for days trying to learn the dance. Once I learned it, I never waste any opportunity to break it down.

This cycle continues for most of the night— I dance like a mad woman, take a break with the slow songs, and get back out there and do it again. All the couples take random breaks but most stay on the dance floor for the slow songs. If I was here with a boyfriend, I would've taken advantage of the opportunity too.

The night is almost over and my feet are killing me. I wore chunky heels to help out with that, but after four hours of dancing, nothing can help. I can't figure out how Amy can handle dancing this entire time in three inch stilettos.

"Mind if I join you?" Alex asks.

"Go for it...but beware...I think my feet are going to spontaneously combust any minute." I laugh in pain. "I think I'm just gonna wear flip-flops to my senior prom."

"Are you at least having fun?" he asks.

"Heck yeah," I yell over the music. "Tons!"

"Me too," he agrees. "This place beats the cafeteria. I feel like I'm in one of those high school movies."

"Yeah...except none of us smuggled in vodka and this isn't a hotel, so I guess the after-prom sex is out of the question," I joke.

"Damn, I forgot about those details," he chuckles.

"Well, it's not like you and Amy need a hotel!" I can't believe I just said that.

"You're crazy Meg..." he laughs. "It's not like that between me and Amy."

"Yeah right," I scoff.

"No, seriously," he says, sincerely. "It's not!"

"You don't have to lie to spare my feelings Alex...I can handle it...it's not like I don't know," I warn.

He turns in his chair and looks in my eyes, "Meg...I don't know where you get your information, but Amy and I are not having sex and we never have...she's only fifteen...you really think that's all I'm interested in, that I'm that kind of guy. You don't know me as well as I thought."

"Why are you lying? I know about the condoms Alex!" I yell.

"What condoms?" Alex cries.

"This stupid act is killing me...Amy and I went to the free teen clinic for birth control. We got the same amount of stuff. I've never used mine but I peeked in her bag and half her stash is gone...so seriously...you don't have to lie!" I turn to look in the other direction.

I can't believe he is trying to lie to me.

"Meg, look at me...look at me please." I turn around and meet his stare. "Listen, I'm not lying to you. Amy wanted to get really physical...she wanted to have sex...but I didn't feel comfortable with that 'cause she's so young. I really care a lot about her, but I'm not ready for that next step and I don't want her to think that just 'cause I'm a senior I'm out for a piece of ass. It's just not my style. I didn't even know you guys got condoms till you just told me."

"Well if you and her aren't having sex, then who is she freakin' screwing?" I demand.

We both look at each other and then look out at the dance floor.

There it is. There is the answer and it has been there for so long.

"It's about time you two figured this shit out!"

We look behind us and there is Ben. This guy is like a freakin' stalker, always lurking around waiting for the right time to talk some shit.

I try to clear my head before I speak, "You knew about this and didn't tell me?"

"Wait a minute. We just barely started talking. You would have never believed me...you would've thought I was just being an asshole. Besides you guys broke up and it didn't matter anymore."

"How long has this been going on?" I ask. "I found out about the condoms at my pool party."

"I don't know when they starting boning...but they were hooking up at the beach...that's why it took them so long to get back. I saw them in the bathroom together," Ben explains.

Alex finally chimes in, "I think something's been going on since the Powder Puff game. They both took off after dumb ass here started talking smack...do you remember? Amy wouldn't answer her phone and neither would Eric...damn Ben, I should have listened to you."

"What...he told you and you didn't do anything!" I yell at Alex.

"I didn't believe him. Why would Eric cheat on you?"

"Because I wouldn't give it up, that's why!" I shout.

"Yeah...well I didn't think Amy would cheat on me and I sure as hell didn't think she'd hook up with your boyfriend."

"Why not? She got with you when she knew I obsessed over you the whole freakin' summer," I say, embarrassed.

"I'm sorry Meg...Alex," Ben says as he walks back to the dance floor.

I look at Alex, his nose is turning red, and tears are welling up in his eyes. It's like a chain reaction. I can't help but tear up.

"This just bites...for both of us," he starts. "I wasn't in love with her or anything...but I did have strong feelings for her...this sucks!"

"You know...I wouldn't even care if Eric cheated on me...but Amy is supposed to be my best friend...that's what kills me the most. I can't be her friend anymore."

I bury my face in Alex's chest and sob. He puts his arms around me and rubs his hands slowly up and down my back. On any other day, this act would have been like a fantasy for me, but today, it's hardly comforting.

"Megan...what they hell? Can't you just get your own boyfriend already?" Amy yells to me. Eric and the rest of our friends are coming up right behind her.

Alex lets go of me and we both stand up. I'm first to speak, "Are you freakin' kidding me?" Tears pour down my eyes. "Don't you even freakin' go there okay, just don't!"

She can't shut her big mouth, she has to push. "Meg, come on...what are you crying about? Alex is with me, not you...so just deal!"

I wipe my tears. I don't want to cry anymore for these jerks. Now, I'm just pissed. "Seriously Amy...seriously...hmmm....Eric was with me and you didn't seem to mind, you freakin' skank!"

Both she and Eric look at us in shock.

"I knew it!" Keesh yells. "You've been hookin' up with Eric since spring break...how could you Amy? We're all best friends!" Tears start to well in her eyes now.

"You know what…let's not do this here. If everyone doesn't mind, let's just get the limo and leave." Alex suggests.

No one objects and we head for the door quietly. I can hear some whispers as we pass by but can't make out what anyone is saying.

Amy tries to get Alex's attention, but he tells her calmly, "Amy…I think it would be best if we just cut ties now…I really don't need·to hear anything else."

Alex walks with me to the limo. We get in and sit next to each other, with Eric and Amy sitting alone at the other end. The limo's a super stretch Excursion so there's plenty of room to shun those assholes.

It's quiet except for some sniffles coming from me, Keesh, and Steph. They're probably just as heartbroken as I am by the realization that one of our best friends could do something like this. The guys stay silent. I feel sorry for Vanessa and Erica because they don't even know us and have to deal with our drama.

I glance over at Alex. He smiles at me. He takes my hand and holds it tightly in both of his. I'm so grateful for his friendship. I know I'll never meet another guy like him for the rest of my life.

"Damn…you guys don't waste any time…look at you holding hands…it's not like you two are innocent in all this," Amy shouts across the limo. Eric just stays quiet. Good boy!

"Amy…shut up!" Keesh yells.

"Amy…I never cheated on you…not once…so you cannot blame this on me," Alex responds, sternly.

How can I possibly stay calm at a time like this? I can't. "Seriously Amy…don't even try to blame me…I'm not the one who was FUCKING MY BEST FRIEND'S BOYFRIEND!" I yell, getting louder and louder. "I hope you don't mind being with a guy that only cares about sex because Eric doesn't care about you….the only reason he hooked up with you is because you were willing to spread your skanky legs when I wouldn't! So just shut the hell up already…before I freakin' rip out your fake freakin' hair! You damn whore!"

I take a deep breath, lean back, exhale, and feel a sense of relief.

The rest of the ride home, the limo is still.

When we get to Steph's house, we all pile out of the limo. I hear Amy get on the phone and ask her parents to pick her up. Keesh and Steph rush to me to see if I'm okay. I assure them I'm fine and apologize for ruining their night.

"Meg, do you want a ride home," Alex asks.

"Sounds good," I hug my friends before Alex and I leave. I'm not in the mood to hash it all out for everyone right now. They're going to have to wait.

"Some night," I mumble, as we drive away.

"Pretty pathetic, huh." He chuckles.

We pull up in front of my house in silence.

"Well I guess we have another thing in common," I mutter. "We both lost something tonight."

He studies me, confused by my comment.

"Yeah…you lost your girlfriend…and I lost my best friend."

32

The news is all over school. The easy freshman cheated on her senior beau with her best friend's man. It pretty much sucks for Amy because she looks really bad any way you look at it. In a few years, people won't remember me or Alex or even Eric, they'll just remember that Amy girl, who was some skanky ho-bag.

I'm okay with that. It's kind of sad that I am but I'm not over it yet. It sucks I lost one of my best friends, but who needs a friend like that? I sure don't.

Everyone called or texted me for the rest of the weekend. Everyone except for Amy—she didn't try to contact any of us—but what could she really say? I explain over and over again that I'm fine, but none of them believe me. I said what I needed to say to Amy in the limo. I'm ready to move on.

School will be a little awkward since we all have so many classes together. Mr. Mitchell is already up on the gossip so when we all arrive in class, he sends Amy on an errand that takes almost the entire period. He's so cool! I need to get to sixth period early to fill Ms. Gelson in with the details. I hope she lets me change seats.

Lunch is weird...I'm not sure what to expect. Amy's probably hanging out with her sister. Maybe Eric even tagged along.

"I'm glad you guys are still here," I say, as I approach our tree. Josh and Jonathan are already there.

"He's whack anyway," Josh says. "We wanna hang with you guys still. Is that cool?"

"Sit down, Grand Slam, you guys aren't goin' anywhere," Keesh says, as she practically tackles Jonathan with a hug.

So it's settled, we'll all still hangout—with the exception of the outcasts, Amy and Eric.

"Do you wanna talk about it Meg," Keesh asks, as she puts her arm around me.

"Not really...but I'm sure you guys are dying to know what happened," I answer. I know I would be.

"We already know...Ben gave us the low down after you and Alex left," Jonathan explains.

"Just so you know...we didn't know anything. If I did I would've told you," Josh adds.

Jonathan snickers, "And I would've slide tackled his ass on the soccer field!"

"Next year, babe...you can get him next year." Keesh smiles at her sweetheart.

"So wassup everybody?" Alex mutters. He sits down across from me on the grass.

I lift my head to look at him. "Not much!"

What the hell am I supposed to say?

"So has anyone talked to Amy or Eric?" Alex questions.

"I talked to Eric," Josh says. "He's a dumb ass. He's pissed 'cause Jon and I still want to hang out with all you guys. He's just gonna have to deal...what he did was stupid."

"Give me a break," Keesha cries. "Guys do that crap all the time!"

"Not all of them," Alex argues.

"And not within a group friend," Jonathan points out.

"Good point!" Keesh agrees.

"Heeeyyy" Steph yells.

Steph and Dominic join us. The guys take turns doing the guy hand shake. Steph sits down next to me, opposite of Keesha. The guys start talking about sports crap and Memorial Day weekend parties.

Steph and Keesh huddle in close to talk to me about Amy.

"So what do you want to do about Amy?" Steph asks.

I don't even have to think about this one. "Nothing."

Keesh jumps in, "Really Meg, you're not going to talk to her?"

"No...I'm really not! There's no excuse for what she did, so what's there to talk about. She could say she's sorry a million times—which you know she won't—and it wouldn't matter. Do you guys really want to be friends with someone like her?" I demand.

"No...not really...I trust Dominic but I wouldn't want her anywhere near him," Steph explains. "I kinda feel bad for her, but I can't stick up for her. You're right. There *is* no excuse."

"This isn't like she broke my favorite earrings or flirted with my boyfriend...she had sex with him...a lot of sex with him...and she still let him kiss me. That just pisses me off and grosses me out!" I hiss.

Ben, Vanessa, and Erica join our little party too. Erica cuddles up to Josh, and Ben and Vanessa plop themselves down near Alex.

"Well," Ben shouts. "Looks like we're all here now! One big happy family!"

We all grin at him and laugh. Family maybe, but happy...that's a stretch.

"No...we're not all here!" Amy yells, tears coming down her eyes.

Keesh swoops to her feet in a split second, "Amy, this isn't a good idea...so just go somewhere else!"

"Meggie, can we talk?" Amy asks me.

Everyone turns my way quickly.

I look up at her and say, "Don't you dare call me Meggie. And no...I don't need to talk to you."

"Come on Meg, don't be like this!" She turns toward Keesh and Steph for support. "What? Are you guys never gonna talk to me again? We've been friends forever...this is it...you're just gonna ditch me!"

Steph stands up. "Meg's not interested in being your friend anymore, and neither am I or Keesh...so you need to go away.

But just remember one thing...we didn't ditch you. You ditched us! Real friends don't do shit like you did...now just go," Steph cries, her hands shaking and her mouth quivering. Dominic swoops up to her side. He puts his hand on her shoulder for comfort.

"Come on Amy...you're just making yourself look more stupid," Jen says to her sister. Where did she come from? She grabs her sister's hand and yanks her away.

Ben mumbles under his breath, "I doubt that's possible." Alex smacks him in the back of his head and tells him to shut up.

Amy stomps off with Jen, leaving us in peace...in silence.

"Well that was fun," Ben exclaims.

33

Memorial Day Weekend is filled with possibilities. Since Prom, everyone has been preoccupied with thoughts and talk about Amy and Eric. It finally seems to be dying down. Amy's parents came to school and convinced her counselor to switch around her schedule—so we don't have all the same classes anymore. For any other student, switching classes at the end of the school year would have been unheard of. But for Amy, the daughter of the president of the school booster club, a schedule change is a piece of cake. The only class that we have the same is ASB, but she found another group of people to kick it with and that's fine with me.

This weekend has given me—and my friends—a chance to start over.

"You guys ready?" Alex asks when I open the door.

"Hi Alex," my mom gushes. "So nice to see you again...you're taking the girls to a party?"

Keesh and I can really use some cheering up too. We just found out that we didn't make the dance team. It's okay though. I kind of expected it. I was so caught up in dealing with Amy that I didn't have my mind right. We still have two more years. Maybe if we do well in intermediate next year, the teacher will bump us up to team. We'll see.

"Hi Mrs. Miller," he gives her a hug. She loves it. "Yeah...we haven't done much since prom so we thought we'd have some fun before we all have to study for finals."

She adores Alex. He could say he's taking me to the mountains to sacrifice me to a cult and she'd be fine with it.

Keesh, Steph, and I pass my mom and are out of the house.

"Bye Mom, love ya!" I shout.

"You all have a great time," she yells to us.

"Bye, Mrs. Miller," Alex calls back to her. "We're gonna lap it so we only have to take one car," Alex explains as he slides open the door to reveal the rest of the crew. Ben, Vanessa, Josh, and Erica are squished in the far back seat of the van. Steph, Keesh, Jonathan, and I take the middle seat, and Alex and Dominic sit in the front. I know Steph wants to sit with Dom, but there's no way he'll fit in the back with three other people, he's even too big for the front.

The party is already crowded when we get there. The guys were hungry so we stopped at Denny's first. I would seriously hate to work there, with high school kids coming in all the time. We aren't the best patrons—we're so loud and obnoxious—always laughing, cussing, and yelling at each other across the table. And we always take a souvenir—a menu, ketchup bottles, silverware. Once, Jonathan actually took a booster seat.

The DJ plays *Walk It Out* as we arrive. It's almost too perfect. We all shake our way to the dance area and got our freak on. That song finishes and the place goes wild with *Get Low*. Everyone's swaying their hands in the air to Lil' Jon's lyrics. The song is so dirty, but I love it. Keesh cracks everyone up as she *backs it up* into Jonathan. The poor guy looks scared. It seems like forever before we take a break. Little by little, some of us migrate from the dance floor to get some drinks.

"You want something?" Alex asks me.

"Yeah...why not...surprise me!" I answer.

I watch as he splits his way through the crowd, and I keep dancing.

"Can you believe the year is almost over," Ben yells into my ear.

"No way." I laugh. "It seems like yesterday that we were at a party and you were trying to get me all liquored up."

He smiles, "Yeah...well, that was a long time ago...I'm sorry I hurt you Meg."

I shout back, "Don't trip...it's all good now."

"Well, I'm glad we're friends again...I'm gonna miss you!" Ben yells.

I laugh. "It's not like you're dying, you're just graduating."

"Don't remind me!" he shouts.

Vanessa and Alex return with drinks in their hand.

"You're not drinking, are you?" I ask Alex.

He rolls his eyes. "I'm Designated Dave...it's a Coke, nerd!"

"Just checking!" I shout, taking a swig of my drink. "Ummm....yummy...a Diet Coke!"

He winks, "Just thought you'd want to *remember* the last party of the year."

I smile at him, hypnotized by his big brown eyes, and we dance for the rest of the night.

The drive-in! I've never been to the drive-in. I didn't realize they still *existed*. Alex texts me to see if I want to go out tonight. I, of course, text him back with a yes. I thought we were just going to go to the movies. But when we get here, it isn't a movie theater...it's a drive-in.

"I brought some popcorn, licorice, Kit-Kats, and a Diet Coke for you and Coke for me," Alex informs me.

"Cool...but didn't I see a snack bar back there?" I ask.

"Yeah...but the line is always long and you end up missing part of the movie."

"This is...interesting," I mutter, as I look around.

"You've never been here before?"

"Nope."

"They show two movies and we'll hear the sound through the radio."

Hmm.

We get situated with snacks and drinks before the movie starts. I unbuckle my seatbelt and move the seat back to get comfortable. I think about how sweet Alex is. He got all my favorite snacks. I've never told him these are my favorite. He's just noticed from all the times we've been around each other. Or maybe they're his favorites too. It doesn't matter. We're here. I'm here...with Alex.

Previews show first and I feel like talking. It's weird because at a movie theater, you know you're not supposed to talk, but here, in Alex's little car, I just want to talk to him.

I look at him and he catches my gaze.

"You know...I've never sat in the front seat with a girl at the drive-in before now," Alex snickers.

"Ooookaaay."

"Usually, I'd be in the backseat all cuddled up already." He chuckles.

"And...you're telling me this, why?"

"I don't know...I have mixed feelings right now."

"Explain," I ask him, curiously.

"Well...you know I have feelings for you Meg. I have for a long time...but I've been holding back," he confesses.

"Why...why would you hold back?"

"Because I'm leaving...I'm graduating," he pauses. "I don't think it would be fair to you to have some college boyfriend while you're in high school."

"So you are leaving," I confirm. "I can't believe we've never talked about this before. I was actually hoping you'd be going to college...since that's my goal. Uhhh, where're you going?"

"Berkeley," he says, confidently. "It's pretty far away...like a nine hour drive. I won't be coming home a lot...only for holidays."

"Oh," I respond, saddened by the news.

"See...that's why we can't be together. You need to experience all the things I did in high school. Well, not all of them. But I don't want to hold you back. If you go to a party and meet someone, I don't want you to have to worry about me. If some guy asks you to homecoming, I want you to go. I can't be here for all that stuff." He trails off.

"Oh...I understand." I want to cry but I don't. I don't want to sound like a baby. I understand what he's saying, but that doesn't make it any easier.

"I really want to be with you, but I just don't think it would be fair...to either one us," he explains.

"So what does this mean? Are you saying we're not gonna be friends anymore?" I ask in almost a whisper.

He touches my face. "No way, we can email, text, call...I'll visit when I come home if you want me to. We just can't be a couple...not *now*!"

"Explain that...*not now*," I ask.

He smirks. "If things work out according to my plan, you'll experience the high school experience, I'll do the same with college...and then someday...if it's meant to be...it'll just happen...we'll be together!"

"Someday huh," I grin.

"Someday."

"So I guess that means you're not going to throw me in the backseat then," I joke.

He chuckles a bit. "Not tonight...anyway."

We gaze at each other in silence.

"Oh wait!" He startles me. "I almost forgot." He grabs a paper bag from the backseat. Oh no, he better not have *lunch* in there. He reaches in slowly and pulls out a small pink box.

"This is for you," he says, with a crooked smile.

"What is it?" I ask, settling it in my lap to open the lid. "Oh my gosh!" It's a cupcake. There is a pink polka dotted candle coming out of the top.

"Happy birthday Meg." he says, reaching over to light the candle.

"How did you know?" I ask, surprised.

"The girls told me. They said your mom usually has a big party for you, but this year you didn't want one. Happy Birthday, make a wish."

I close my eyes, make a wish, and softly blow out the candle.

"Thank you, Alex."

I lean over and hug him. We hold each other close for a minute and then let go with a big sigh. He takes my hand. "Is this okay?" We look down at our intertwined hands.

"Yup."

For the rest of the night, we watch the two movies, hand in hand, only taking a break to drink or eat something. After each break, he grasps my hand again like we're magnets being pulled together.

This is enough...for now.

34

Stores are filled with graduation balloons, cards, little stuffed animals, etc. The school year is over and there isn't anything I can do to stop Alex from graduating tonight. I'm pretty sure my grades went down—I couldn't focus on studying for finals. Everyone in our tight-knit crew of friends feels the exact same way, none us want to see the seniors go. I don't think they want to leave us.

There's something magical that happened the night of Prom. While it pretty much sucked, the results have been so much better. Keesh, Steph, and I have become pretty good friends with Vanessa and Erica. Vanessa has turned out to be a lot nicer than I thought she was. I guess I shouldn't have judged her by her pom-poms. Josh and Jonathan have also become tight with Dominic, Ben, and Alex.

Next year, things are going to be so different. Alex is headed up north to Berkeley. Ben, Vanessa, and Erica are staying close at a community college. At least, we can see them anytime if we want to. Emails and phones calls will have to do for Alex and I.

Keesh, Steph, and I convinced Mr. Mitchell to let us all in the stadium for graduation. There is no way we could score enough tickets, so being in ASB helped us out again. It's not so bad being a "Double Threat". There have definitely been some perks to go along with this title.

We anxiously wait for our friends to walk out as *Pomp and Circumstance* comes through the speakers. It's a huge graduating class of four hundred students. And there they are: Ben first, then Vanessa, Erica, and last, Alex.

Tears stream lightly down my cheeks. I'm so happy and so sad at the same time.

"This is going to be us in three years," Steph screeches.

We quiet down with the rest of the crowd to listen to the graduation speeches and all the rest of the crap that goes with it. Who really cares about all the formalities? We just want to see them get their diplomas. When the time finally comes, the graduates stand up row by row, and march toward the stage.

"Here they come," Keesh squeals.

"Ben Calloway," the counselor calls. We scream.

"Vanessa Reyes," she crosses the stage. We scream again.

"Erica Martinez."

Josh yells, "Yeah, Erica!"

"Alex Aguilar," he takes his diploma, looks up at us, and winks.

We scream, yell, and clap some more.

We try to settle down after our friends cross the field.

"Now what?" Jonathan asks.

Dominic answers, "Ben said to meet them by the buses so they can say bye before they go to grad night."

"Let's go then," I stand up to leave.

"Don't you want to see them turn their tassels?" Steph stops me.

We wait and cheer them on again. I'm very anxious to get to the buses. I'm dying to see Alex. I know I'll see him during the summer, but for some reason, tonight makes everything seem so final. I feel like it's all over...once he gets on that bus...it's...it's all up to fate!

"Let's go," I instruct everyone as I start to make my descent down the bleachers. The crew follows as I head out toward the buses.

"Chill Meggie," Keesh says. "They'll probably be awhile. They still have to see their parents and take pictures and all that crap."

Oh, I forgot about that.

It isn't too long before I hear Dominic yell, "Congratulations, Man!"

The hugs begin as each of us take our turn congratulating all the graduates.

"When do you guys leave?" I ask Alex.

Just then Mr. Mitchell shouts into the bullhorn, "Graduates, you need to get on the buses, we leave in five minutes."

Alex shrugs his shoulders. I look up at him. Everyone else is invisible now.

"Did you bring it?" he asks.

"Yup!" I say, a single tear falling down my cheek.

He wipes my tear and we exchange yearbooks.

He throws his arms around me, squeezing me tightly. He pulls back, and then gazes in my eyes. And then…and then…he kisses me. Not just a peck either! A passionate kiss like the ones I've read about in my mom's romance novels. His breath *is* sweet. Our lips join perfectly, fitting together like puzzle pieces. He slowly pulls away again before planting a few gentle kisses on my lips and finally one last peck on my forehead where he lingers for a few seconds. Perfect. He hugs me again and whispers in my ear, "I'll be thinking of you."

We're interrupted by cheers and clapping.

"Wooohoo!"

"Get it girl!"

"Alright, Alex!"

"It's about time!"

"Yeaahhhh!"

We turn to look at our friends and we laugh.

He hugs me one last time before joining Ben, Vanessa, and Erica to get on the bus.

I watch them board. I watch the bus pull away.

I open my yearbook to the Backward's page, the one with a huge picture of Alex on it in his crown. I knew this is where he'd write. I'm not surprised to see that *one* special word scrawled out in his writing, because I wrote the same thing to him.

Someday...All My Love, Alex

We don't need to say anything else.

Someday...

Acknowledgements

There are many people—family, friends, and colleagues—that I would like to thank for their undying support and enthusiasm for *So I'm A Double Threat*.

First, much love and thanks to my husband, James, and my children, Corey, Vanessa, Samantha, and Sara, for humoring me in this endeavor. James, thank you so much for the encouragement and always believing in me. Corey and Ness, thanks for helping me with the voice of a teenager. Samantha and Sara, thank you for giving up so much time with mom. I doubt I will ever be famous enough to help you meet the Jonas Brothers, but maybe we can hit a concert.

To Sylvie, you're a reader now! I'm proud. Thanks so much for reading this book chapter by chapter and motivating me to keep writing. I loved getting text messages from you with predictions such as "Amy and Eric are having lunch, aren't they?" You have been an inspiration.

To Pam, a simple thank you is not enough. You were such a great supporter of this project from the very beginning. Thanks so much for reading the entire manuscript in its roughest version and helping me revise. I truly value your opinion, and all the suggestions that you made. I am so grateful for all you do.

To my brother, Mark, for landing me my first TV appearance. I can't wait. Well, I guess I'm going to have to write a picture book if I want you to read my work. Until then, you will have to stick with Tucker Max.

Finally, to my mom, Dolores, and my sister, Monica, who have told anyone who will listen about this book. You have always been some of my biggest cheerleaders for everything I do, along with Dad. In his absence, there have been giant shoes to fill in that cheering section and you have not let me down.

Thanks for listening to and reading my chapters over and over. Without your encouragement, I'm not sure I would've finished. I love you!

I would like to express my gratitude and appreciation to the following people for their support, many of whom read the entire manuscript and gave me suggestions, or may have been the *constant* little bird in my ear encouraging me to finish:

Juanita Prestsater, Amy Scherbarth, Daniel Davis, Annie Marin (& Uncle Pete), Kristen Gracia, Genevieve Brown, Dr. Jan Pilgreen, Joni Siegel, Melissa Dietzman, Cindy Beck, Kristine Sweet, Alegria Arizaga, Christian Ceballos, Nimsi Velasco, Jasmine Pinones, Philip Siegel, and:

Daniel Van Beek—my cover is awesome!

Adriana Pilonieta—thanks for taking a million pics of me

My Original Dannytown Girls—Kim, Angie, Jaime, Shawn, Amanda, Bev, Irene, Natasja, Claire, Carolyn, Jenai, Laura, Stephanie, Karen, Wendy, Lisa, Erika, Naomi, Heatherlynn, Heather, Amy, Sharon, and Lilli—ODT Rocks!

Club Click—Liza, Claudia, and Cheri

JoJo Wright—Thanks for allowing me to use the Question of the Night

The We've Got Soul Book Club—Sylvie, Teri, Ellen, Shazia, Sarah, Andrea, Edita, and Stephanie—or as Eric would call them, the MILFS!

About The Author

Julie Prestsater loved high school so much that she went back as a science teacher and currently teaches reading. Julie never enjoyed reading in high school. In fact, the only book she ever read cover to cover was *The Day I Became An Autodidact* by Kendall Hailey, assigned by Mr. Norm Rush during her junior year of honors English. She credits her love for reading now to her instructor, Monica MacAuley, who assigned the Biobag project in a children's literature class at the University of La Verne.

With only three books—Haliey's, *Speak* by Laurie Halse Anderson, and *Are You There God It's Me Margaret* by Judy Blume—to fill her biobag that was to trace her life through literature, Julie embarked on a search for books or genres that interested her. Throughout the semester, she read book after book, falling in love with chica lit authors Mary Castillo and Alisa Valdes-Rodriguez, the Heather Wells Series by Meg Cabot, *Summer Sisters* by Judy Blume, anything by Jerry Spinelli, Laurie Halse Anderson, or Jodi Picoult, and of course, the Harry Potter series. She is not afraid to admit that she waited in line for a few hours for the midnight release of the *Deathly Hallows*. "The biobag project changed my life," she says.

Julie is convinced that it only takes one good book to metamorphose a reluctant reader, such as herself, into a life-long reader.

This is Julie's first novel. The sequel titled *Double Threat My Bleep*, and a standalone novel, *You Act So White*, will be available in the fall of 2010.

Visit her on the Web at www.juliepbooks.com.

Made in the USA
Charleston, SC
16 May 2011